'Is she fit to
late in the d
Pete shrug to
check it out.'
'Do it on th Blair, making
for the flight de getting the hell out of
here.'

'Now?' Pete looked up in amazement.

'Now. Stand by for the fastest pre-flight check ever.'

'Where's your freight?'

'Still in the sheds,' said Blair. 'And that's where it's staying.' He was already in the left-hand seat, buckling on his harness.

'Where's the ground crew?' asked Pete. 'There's no one to handle the GPU.'

'Forget the GPU,' snapped Blair. 'I'm starting her on the batteries.' Straight ahead, through the screen, he could see the tank, squatting in his path like an iron toad, its cannon still pointing straight at the Britannia's nose.

Eric Paice

BUCCANEER

ARROW BOOKS

Arrow Books Limited
3 Fitzroy Square, London W1P 6JD

An imprint of the Hutchinson Publishing Group

London Melbourne Sydney Auckland
Wellington Johannesburg and agencies
throughout the world

First published 1980

Set in Monotype Times

Made and printed in Great Britain
by The Anchor Press Ltd
Tiptree, Essex

ISBN 0 09 923430 0

1

The digital clock in the airport lounge showed 0500. Central African time. Captain Blair stood at the plate-glass window looking out across the single, makeshift runway as the first light of dawn streaked the sky. At the far end, near some tumbledown shacks that housed cargo and customs offices, stood the fat-bellied four-engine Bristol Britannia freight plane he had brought into Ximbali the previous evening. On the perimeter of the tarmac, two young black soldiers sat listlessly, sleepily, their Uzi sub-machine-guns propped up against their knees. And beyond them, an endless dark forest that stretched a hundred miles to the border. Outside the terminal building, between the passenger lounge and the apron, half a dozen more soldiers had erected a hastily built firebase of sand-bags and packing crates. They too were suffering the exhaustion of an overnight march to protect their country's one commercial air strip from insurgents. And at the opposite end of the runway, its long tapered snout pointing directly down the tarmac towards the Britannia, squatted a fat Centurion tank.

Blair turned to Don Saunders.

'I think it's time we got out of here, son.'

The young co-pilot smiled, eyed the tank and the sleepy soldiers and asked quietly, 'Can you make it?'

Blair looked again towards the menacing tank.

'Unladen, and in cool air, with about six feet to spare.'

Both men knew that the air temperature was crucial. Within an hour the tarmac would be shimmering with heat and the hotter the outside temperature, the less lift from the Britannia's four Proteus 255 turbo-props. No chance then of clearing that fat, ugly tank with even an inch to spare.

'How about that lot?' said Saunders as a young corporal from the Ximbali National Guard stood up for a moment to stretch his limbs and shake the sleep from his eyes.

'With a bit of luck,' said Blair quietly, 'they won't catch on till we're halfway down the strip.'

Saunders tried to look convinced.

'Are you game?' asked the older man.

'You're the skipper,' said the younger man. He shrugged and told himself he was not afraid.

Both men turned away from the window and started to stroll casually towards a door leading to the airport lounge toilets.

Monica Burton watched them approach. Stretched out on the vinyl-covered bench, she had woken a few minutes earlier to wonder, momentarily, what in God's name she was doing in this flyblown lounge, arms and legs numb and eyelids gummed up with sleep. She had been watching the backs of the two men in their crumpled aircrew uniforms, the older man tall and broad, the younger slim and freckle-faced. They looked safe. Certain of what they were doing. She smiled at Blair and hoped for contact.

He smiled back and passed on by.

She looked around at the other passengers stranded in the lounge. The two young men who formed her camera crew were still dead to the world, their Mitchell camera, tripod and sound equipment stacked neatly at their feet. On a nearby bench two middle-aged businessmen snored loudly, their mouths hung open in exhaustion. A younger man in a light tropical suit with a two-day growth of beard raised his head from his brown briefcase pillow and fumbled for a cigarette.

All in the same boat. Soon they would be up and around asking each other the questions they knew none could answer. No help there.

She called across to the two aircrew men as they reached the exit doors. 'Will there be any more planes out of here?'

'Doesn't look like it,' Blair called back and smiled his easy smile. 'If I were you I'd head back to town and find the consul's office.'

No help there, either.

'Should we have offered her a lift?' asked Saunders as they climbed out through the toilet window and dropped silently on to the verge at the back of the terminal building.

'Too chancy,' said Blair.

'She was dishy,' said the co-pilot.

'I know,' said Tony Blair, who didn't normally pass a woman in distress without a second glance. But this time he would have to let it go.

They walked casually, easily down the airport approach road towards the forest fringe as though they were out for a Sunday walk. As they reached the cover of the trees and began to work their way around the perimeter of the airfield towards the Britannia, Blair began to suffer a twinge of guilt. Perhaps he should have offered to take the stranded passengers. They were British – the girl, anyway, he had no knowledge of the others, or indeed where any of them had come from. Blair cared too much for Africa to be a white supremacist, but still retained a vague feeling that in the turmoil of this explosive black continent the whites should stick together in a crisis. Or was this simply an ancient clan instinct from his Highland ancestry?

Perhaps, as Saunders suggested, he should just have taken the blonde. Her nine-odd stone of weight would scarcely make any difference to his maximum take-off weight. On the other hand he had no right to place her in any greater danger than she was in already. Although the Ximbali National Guard were not a trigger-happy bunch in normal times, they did have a revolution on their hands, and no doubt their local commander, having given orders to close the airport to all traffic, would also have given orders to shoot anyone who disobeyed it. He glanced again at the ugly tank at the far end of the runway. Even if it was only manned by semi-trained farm boys, they could hardly miss a plane the size of a Brit hurtling down the tarmac towards them.

In fact, the more Blair thought about it, the more he realized it was a mad, stupid, totally reckless bloody gamble anyhow. But he had to be back in the UK by nightfall. Too much was at stake. . . .

Further speculation came to an abrupt halt. He was staring down the barrel of a blunt-nosed Uzi. Another was levelled at Saunders' throat. Neither had seen the two black soldiers step out silently from cover. No one said a word for what seemed like an agonizingly long time. Don Saunders tensed and swallowed on a dry throat. Blair felt the sweat breaking out on his forehead. He looked hard into the eyes of the guard as he would a fierce dog. Hold the contact. Never show fear. Smile. Slowly, warmly, but not in such a way as to show contempt. These were no more than boys, no more than sixteen perhaps. But no less dangerous for that. Teenage boys with deadly weapons are prone to shoot first and reason afterwards, such is the lethal impetuosity of youth.

'Just going to inspect our plane. OK?' In English. He tried again in French. Then in a few half-remembered words of Swahili.

If the soldiers understood any of it, they gave no sign.

Slowly, careful to make no sudden movement that would tighten a nervous finger on a trigger, Blair eased his hand to his inside pocket and took out his wallet. It was stuffed two inches thick with paper money. High-denomination notes. Fuel money for a continent where any pilot of a tramp cargo plane knows he may have to pay cash on the nail. The soldiers watched him, expressionless as he peeled off a dozen hundred US dollar notes one by one, then, leaning forward, gently stuffed them into one of the boy's tunic pocket. The Uzi still pointed unwaveringly at

Blair's face. He tried sterling. Another thousand in twenties, finally his remaining Belgian francs.

Then the boy moved. He brought the gun muzzle sharply down on Blair's hand so the wallet dropped to the ground. A moment later both guards smiled. Huge, white teeth smiles, not of pleasure or even gratitude, but simple straightforward amusement as though the whole episode had been a tremendous joke. One of them lowered his gun at last, crouched down to pick up the wallet and a moment later both had dissolved into the forest.

'Kids,' said Saunders, to exorcize his fear.

They stepped out on to the tarmac. The Britannia was now only fifty yards away, the steps still in position, the main freight door still open. The huge silver letters along the hull spelt RED-AIR.

'That's the fuel money gone west,' said Blair. 'Ray Mason's going to love me for that.' Red-Air was Mason's company.

'How do we get home on the fuel?' asked Saunders.

'There's enough to take us over the border.'

'And then?'

'You're walking too fast,' said Blair. 'Keep it nice and casual.'

They kept to the far side of the plane so that it acted as a screen between them and the distant air terminal. Under the body of the plane, then, still casually, up the steps to the hold. No one else appeared to have spotted them.

But this was the easy bit.

Inside, Pete, the flight engineer and third member of the Britannia crew, looked up in surprise. Some reckon the flight engineers have the lousiest job of all the aircrew. Well, Pete did, anyway. A slight, balding man in his mid-thirties, he had a natural hangdog expression. This morning he had more reason for it than any. The Red-Air Britannia was an old plane, built in 1959 for the Royal Air Force, sold off in the mid-seventies when the RAF maintenance men considered it already past its prime and flown consistently ever since on commercial air-freight routes. It had so many new replacement parts you could hardly find the original skeleton. Amazingly, it still managed to scrape past its Certificate of Airworthiness, no one was ever quite sure how, for every time a pilot gave it a hard landing it rattled like a bone cart. And Tony Blair had been forced to give it a nasty jolt on touchdown the night before. Skilled pilot that he was, there isn't much anyone can do when your wheels hit a pothole and you have to slam the engines into reverse in a hurry. The result, as Pete said pithily, was a bad gutsache. Somewhere in the bowels a hydraulic line had come adrift and he had been forced to spend the night tracking it down.

Blair asked, 'Is she fit to fly?'

It was a bit late in the day for that question, but he knew Pete was one of the best flying spanners in the business. There was nothing he couldn't patch up given time.

Pete shrugged. 'I need another half-hour to check it out.'

'Do it on the startup,' shouted Blair, as he made for the flight deck. 'We're getting the hell out of here!'

'Now?' Pete looked up in amazement.

'Now,' said Blair. 'Stand by for the fatest pre-flight check ever.'

'Where's your freight?'

'Still in the sheds,' said Blair, 'and that's where it's staying.'

He was already in the left-hand seat, buckling on his harness.

'Where's the ground crew?' asked Pete. 'There's no one to handle the GPU.'

'Forget the GPU,' snapped Blair. 'I'm starting her on the batteries.'

He flicked the switch to turn the propeller blades to superfine, so cutting down on the air resistance for the start.

Straight ahead he could see the tank, squatting in his

path like an iron toad, its cannon still pointing straight at the Britannia's nose.

Twenty yards into the forest, well out of sight of any prowling officer, the two young Ximbali soldiers squatted down to examine their prize.

They shared the money out equally, not knowing how or where they would ever be able to change it without raising suspicion. But at least these strange foreign banknotes would make splendid souvenirs. Then they emptied the rest of the wallet and examined the Diners Card, Barclaycard, American Express Card and Blair's membership card of the British Airline Pilots' Association with excited curiosity, dividing the spoils between them. Just as they were considering who was entitled to become a member of the Stanwick Airport Golf Club and who the recipient of one pair of cavalry-twill trousers, two blue shirts and a pair of yellow silk pyjamas from the Sunlight Laundry, they died. Both neatly stitched by bullets from a Cuban copy of a Russian version of the American M16. The Angel of Death knows no frontiers.

A few moments later, 300 members of the Ximbali People's Liberation Army, in shabby green uniforms and armed to the teeth, burst out from the forest from a dozen different directions to save their emerging country from the corrupting influence of Western decadence in a murderous crossfire.

It took the stranded passengers in the airport lounge several minutes to realize the airport was under attack. Partly because they were simultaneously being assured by the BBC World Service via Monica Burton's transistor radio that the Ximbali insurrection had failed and the rebels were in full retreat towards the border. A fragment from a mortar shell shattered both their illusions and the plate-glass window. As they hurled themselves to the floor a Katushya rocket hit the flat roof of the building, skimmed like a flat pebble on a pond and buried itself in the control tower which a moment later was a sheet of flames.

One of the camera team, with an instinctive bravery born of professional instinct, suddenly got up, grabbed his Mitchell and ran out on to the apron to try to film the attack. The others, bewildered by the suddenness of the onslaught, ran after him. Any movement was better than lying crouched on the floor of the lounge waiting for the ceiling to crash down on them.

Then, suddenly, over the harsh rattle of sub-machine-gun fire and flat, sickening thud of rocket shells came the distant roar of aircraft engines.

'The bastards,' screamed Monica Burton. 'They knew!'

Hell hath no fury like a woman abandoned, and totally oblivious to the flying bullets she started to run like a scorched cat towards the main runway. That fat, ugly cargo plane out there, already shuddering with power like a wild animal on a leash, was, she knew, their only slim lifeline. She would stop it somehow if she had to stand, waving and screaming, in its path.

Don Saunders slipped the nose chock then, ducking beneath the slipstream from the turbo-props, reached the ladder and clambered up. Kicking it away as he reached the safety of the forward belly hold, he swung the entry door closed, locked it into place, then hurried through to the flight deck. As he climbed into the first officer's seat, Blair and the flight engineer were already on the tail end of the after-start check. Blair looked calm, totally relaxed, even more so than when they had crossed the tarmac together.

'Supercharger airflow . . .'

'Normal,' said the spanner, just as calm as his pilot now they were into the set instrument-check routine. Don Saunders now realized for the first time that the punctilous question and answer routine laid down by regulations not only served to ensure the safety of the plane but, by concentrating the mind on ordinary routine matters, also helped to create an atmosphere of confidence and calm in a crisis.

'Electrical check . . .'

'Complete,' said the flight engineer.

Saunders peered through the windscreen. The tank was still sitting there immobile, presumably awaiting an order to move. The control tower was now a burnt-out skeleton. Rebel troops had already seized the firebase and were fanning out across the airfield. The government troops were desperately trying to regroup under fire.

'Taxi clearance?' asked Pete. The final check on the card.

'You've got to be joking!' grinned Blair. And released the parking brakes.

The Britannia, suddenly unleashed, leapt forward, starting its take-off run.

And in that split second he saw the blonde figure, hair streaming behind her, racing towards the plane. A few yards behind her were the others.

Monica screamed. A futile, absurd scream, from deep in her lungs. 'Stop, for God's sake. Stop!'

As though the Britannia captain, locked behind a wall of noise from the roaring motors, could possibly hear her.

She fell, sprawled helplessly out on the baked earth at the edge of the runway. Her shoulders started to heave in a violent sob.

Then the two cameramen were each side of her, dragging her to her feet.

She pushed away the hair from her eyes, dank with tears, looked up and saw the huge bulk of the plane standing on the runway thirty feet away, and smelt the burning rubber from its tyres. The cargo door was swinging open, a cargo net heaved over the side. Five long minutes later, a sweating Don Saunders had pulled the last of them to safety in the hold. Saunders and Pete quickly rigged the net to the retaining hooks in the fuselage roof so that it was draped down and attached firmly to the floor.

Blair entered from the flight deck. 'We're not equipped

to carry passengers,' he said, still with his easy smile, 'and I don't want you to upset my trim. So spread out, arms above your heads and hang on to that net. OK?'

The second attempt at take-off was even hairier than the first. The sudden stop had used up a hundred yards of runway, but there was no time now to turn back and take it from the top again. Blair held it for as long as he dared on the brakes while he pushed the engine revs, then took off like a rocket from a launcher. The moment the wheels had left the ground he swung up the tricycle undercarriage. He still wouldn't have made it but for the fact that the tank crew finally decided they had better start earning their pay by joining in the battle for the airport and trundled slowly off the runway. The Britannia's starboard wing cleared the turret by what Don Saunders later estimated to be about five millimetres.

Blair levelled the plane off at 20,000 feet, handed over to Don and walked back through the narrow passage from the flight deck to the hold. The two middle-aged businessmen were still clinging to the cargo net like monkeys. Blair told them they could relax now.

'There's coffee in the galley if anyone cares to make it.'

He looked automatically at Monica, squatting against the aircraft fuselage.

Typical, thought Monica, even though they'd all been through the same wringer, when the crisis is over, it's the woman who has to make the coffee. Nevertheless, she got up and reluctantly followed him to the tiny galley.

He took down a tin of instant coffee, dried milk and plastic cups from the cupboards and showed her how to work the water heater. She watched his easy movements, studied the set of his jaw, the network of lines around his eyes, the touch of grey at the temples. A strong face that looked as though it had been shotblasted. Around forty-five, she reckoned. Big-boned, well-built and still only the hint of a belly. A cool man, probably an ice-cold man, yet the smile belied it.

'You saved our lives,' she said finally. 'How can I thank you?'

'Oh,' said Blair casually, 'we'll think of something.'

'I haven't had a chance to ask where you're going.'

'UK.'

'Fine,' she said. 'So are we.'

'What were you doing in Ximbali, anyway? It's not exactly on the main tourist route.'

'Filming wild life,' Monica said.

Blair laughed. 'They certainly laid it on for you at the airport. Life doesn't get much wilder than that.'

The galley was so narrow he had to squeeze past her. He took a little longer than he need, his body pressed up against her. She felt warm, comforted after the terrors of her ordeal. Back there on the tarmac when she had thought this man was going to leave them there to die she had cursed him to hell. Now she wanted to throw her arms round his neck.

She looked up into his face. 'I thought you were going to abandon us,' she said.

'I was, originally.' That was honest, at least.

'What made you change your mind?'

'I thought you were going to run under my wheels. It would have thrown me off course.' He smiled again. She couldn't tell whether this was the truth or not.

'Did you know the rebels were going to attack at daybreak? Is that why you slipped away?'

'I didn't even know there was a bloody war on till I landed there last night,' he said. 'I got out in a hurry because otherwise I could have been stuck there for weeks, and my guv'nor wants his plane back. It's the only one he's got.'

That wasn't strictly true either. Tony Blair had a more urgent and more personal reason for getting back to the UK.

Ten miles short of the Nigerian border, the plane turned west and headed out to sea. From there on they hugged the coast till they reached the seaport town of Cotonou in Benin, or Dahomey as Blair still thought of it until the change of name with self-government. He would have preferred to refuel at Lagos, but knew they'd never let him in. Nigerian Air Traffic Control is very strict. Airlines are allocated slot times – periods when they are allowed to land and take off. Anyone trying to land outside their allocated slot time would be told smartly to clear off out to sea. Apart from that, Blair hadn't even had time to request permission to overfly Nigerian territory, let alone land. Had he attempted it without clearance the crew stood a fair chance of being slapped into jail and held until they could find the money to pay a heavy fine. Strictly speaking, this also applied to Benin, but Blair had flown in and out of Cotonou many times before and had made friends in high places. The other advantage of Cotonou was that in the days when it had been a French colonial town they had established a major phone and telegraph service to Europe. Immediately after landing, Blair called Berner Radio to link him with Stanwick. His problems were by no means over.

The Red-Air Freight offices at Stanwick airport were not exactly salubrious: two ten-year-old Portakabins, a lean-to shack for aircraft spares, half an old hangar and a parking spot on the cargo apron was the extent of Ray Mason's tiny empire. And even these were on short lease.

Air freight is the Cinderella of the airline business. Offices, sheds and planes are usually tucked away out of sight in what might be called the downtown end of every airport. The larger freight companies, of course, also have front offices up at the smart end. That's where they keep the pretty girls and the IBM typewriters. But Ray Mason wasn't in that league. At one time he had dreams of becoming another Freddy Laker or Mike Keegan, the boss of Transmeridian. But somehow or other things hadn't quite worked out that way. Mason claimed that he had come into the business ten years too late. Both Laker and Keegan had started at the end of the war when planes and spares could be bought for next to nothing from RAF surplus. Then came the Berlin airlift when any old crate that could leave the ground was pressed into service. And in those days, Mason would say enviously, they let you get on with the business of flying. These days it was all paperwork, regulations, forms to fill up in triplicate, Common Market edicts and Value Added Tax, the most monstrous of all European instruments of torture ever to be imported. Deep in his subconscious, Mason knew there were other reasons why he had not turned his company into a major carrier, but they were too painful to admit, so he put it down to bad luck.

Abrasive on the surface, Ray Mason was, in reality, a kind man, loyal to his friends and generous to a fault, though he tried hard to suppress these qualities by aggression. Stocky, powerfully built, his health was not as good as his frame suggested. When he arrived at the office that morning he was already having trouble from his spare ulcer.

Kim Hayward, his assistant, handed him the phone.

'Captain Blair's on the line from Cotonou,' she told him.

'What's the silly bugger doing there?'

Kim explained what had happened, then handed the phone to her boss.

When Blair told him he needed cash to pay his landing fees and buy fuel, Mason blew his top.

'I gave you ten grand for that trip, if you've blown it that's your lookout, you can bloody walk home!'

When he had finally calmed down he told Blair there was no way he could get cash out to him in less than twenty-four hours, even if he had it to spare. Then he started leading off about the lost cargo until he found he was talking into a dead instrument. Blair had hung up on him.

'Won't one of the local agents give him credit?' asked

Don Saunders as they walked back to the aircraft.

'Ray Mason? He'd be lucky to get credit off his milkman,' replied Blair.

'So what are we supposed to do? Sit it out on Cotonou airfield?'

'We can't. I've got to be back by nightfall, one way or the other.'

It was Monica Burton who got them out of trouble with a phone call to London. She had also made another phone call, but Blair didn't know about that.

Six hours later, as the Britannia started its landing run into Stanwick, he said to his co-pilot: 'Listen, if anyone wants to know who flew this crate out of Ximbali, it was you, OK?'

'Where were you then?' Saunders asked.

'At home in my bed.'

When the plane was safely parked and the shutdown checks completed, Blair grabbed his log and Jepperson charts and made for the door. Monica and the rest of the rescued passengers hurried over to grab his hand and thank him, but he brushed them aside. The moment the steps were up he started to run down them two at a time. He was halfway across the apron when the newsmen came running towards him, cameras flashing in the gathering dusk, reporters clamouring to ask him questions. He charged through the throng like an angry bull.

Mason was waiting with a car. As they piled in, Blair turned on him in fury. 'Did you lay those bastards on?'

'No, mate. But there was nothing I could do. Someone phoned the story through from Benin. You're a bleedin' hero, whether you like it or not.'

'Shit!' said Blair.

The car sped off the tarmac.

Fifteen minutes later, a chauffeur-driven Daimler pulled rapidly away from Stanwick air terminal. In the back was a dishevelled, exhausted but strangely exhilarated Monica Burton. The man beside her, a dapper man in his early forties in a dark Savile Row suit, put his arm around her.

'I was worried sick about you, darling,' Charles Burton said.

'I was in perfectly good hands, Charles,' she answered with a touch of smugness.

'Who was he?' Charles asked.

'I don't know,' she said. 'He didn't give his name and the rest of the crew wouldn't tell me.'

'How very odd,' said her husband in his impeccable City accent.

Dennis Harper, chief personnel officer for Trans-Africa Airlines, glanced through the pile of newspapers on his desk, then passed one of them to Senior Staff Captain Middleton. Middleton, an iron-grey man in his late fifties, studied it, then shook his head more in sorrow than in anger.

There was a knock on the door and Blair entered. A very different Blair. No longer the rough-and-ready air-cargo pilot, but impeccably dressed in the smart, gold-trimmed uniform of a passenger airline captain. He knew both the senior staff men well – had known them for years. He also knew he was in deep trouble.

'Morning, Dennis,' he said breezily. And to Middleton, 'Hullo, Frank, how's it going?'

They nodded silently. Neither smiled.

'Take a seat, Tony,' said Harper ominously.

The captain eased his long legs into a Parker Knoll.

'I imagine you've seen the morning papers,' Harper picked up a copy of the *Guardian* and read the headline on the front-page second-lead story as though it was bad news. 'Skyfreighter in dramatic rescue bid.' He put it aside and picked up the *Telegraph*. 'Hero of Ximbali.'

The *Sun* had given it the whole of the cover page. Harper went on reading, his voice carefully neutral. 'Daredevil freighter captain snatches blonde from African hellhole.' There was a picture of Blair on the apron at Stanwick and another of Monica Burton.

'It's all rubbish,' said Blair with a self-deprecating gesture.

'Buccaneer Blair,' Harper read from the *Mirror*.

So they'd found out his name. Blair now knew the chips were down.

'I did try to keep my name out of it,' he said lamely.

'Buccaneer Blair!' Middleton savoured the tag as though it was a claret he wasn't quite sure of. Then, with a hint of irony, 'You're going to get stuck with that one, Tony.'

'You must have known you'd never get away with it,' Harper said.

There was a moment's silence as they waited for Blair to present his excuse – if he had one.

'All right. I was unlucky. I got caught in a revolution. It could happen to anyone.'

'Quite,' said Harper thinly. 'But if it's going to happen to a senior captain in our fleet we'd prefer him to be flying one of *our* aircraft . . . for which he draws his salary.'

Blair said, 'I'm sorry. I was just doing a favour for a friend.'

'You were moonlighting!' Middleton snapped.

'I said I was sorry, Frank. . . .'

'You're sorry you got caught!'

'How long have you been flying for this tramp-cargo cowboy on the side?' Harper asked.

'Occasionally,' said Blair vaguely.

And then they let him have it for the next ten minutes. Did the Civil Aviation Authorities know what he was up to? Had he exceeded the 200 hours a month laid down in the regulations?

Blair hadn't. He was always careful to keep on the right side of the all-powerful CAA who would take any pilot's licence away without a second thought. But it was about the only crime he hadn't committed in the airline's book. He was under exclusive contract to fly jumbos for Trans-Africa. When stood down, awaiting a flight, he should have been resting like any other pilot, not slipping away to hump cargo for some ramshackle tramp outfit.

There was a touch of scorn in Harper's voice when he said this. Blair knew the snobbery in the airline business. Passenger captains are the *crème de la crème*. They have an image to keep up. It was like a Rolls-Royce chauffeur earning a few bob on the side by driving a coal truck as far as they were concerned. Middleton knew he wasn't the only one of the captains under his wing to have done a bit of moonlighting on the side, but they had always been discreet, turning up promptly for their proper scheduled flights and mainly sinning far afield and in silence. But there was no way of turning the other cheek on this one. The press had been on all morning, probing for the dirt behind the news. They had had to pretend Blair had special permission to fly for someone else, but a sharp reporter would soon get at the truth, then it would appear that Trans-Africa didn't pay their senior pilots a living wage. Which wasn't true and would only give the airline a bad image.

'For Christ's sake, Tony! You don't need the money. Or were you just fiddling your tax? If so, I hope they clobber you!'

'That's my business,' Blair said stubbornly.

He looked at his watch. They'd done their job and torn him off a strip. Fair enough.

'I've got a Rome flight in an hour.'

'I've put a standby captain on for that flight,' said Middleton. 'You're grounded.'

Blair had been half expecting it. They were bound to punish him. 'How long for?' He expected a couple of weeks, a month perhaps at the outside.

Harper looked at him steadily.

'Tony,' he said slowly, more in sorrow than in anger, 'you're a fine pilot. One of the best and most experienced in the fleet. If we could have covered for you, we would have done, but it's out of our hands. The Old Man has asked for a full report. There's plenty of younger men waiting for that left-hand seat. There's no knowing what action he may decide to take, but you'd better prepare yourself for the worst.'

Blair's heart sank. He knew that if Trans-Africa fired him it wouldn't be easy to find another passenger carrier, not at his age and with a black mark against his record. As he reached the door, Middleton put a hand on his shoulder. Before retiring to a desk job, Frank Middleton had been a serving pilot himself and knew what the other man must be thinking.

'That was a neat bit of flying, Tony,' he said quietly.

Monica rolled out of bed, stood on tiptoe, stretched and yawned like a cat. She showered, soaping her slim body luxuriously. At thirty-one she still enjoyed the feel of her own flesh. Small breasts, but still firm. Stomach taut. Thighs just thickening slightly, but soft, yielding. A faint tracery of blue lines behind the knees would one day become varicose. But not yet. Not for a long time yet. No children. Yet. What sheer joy to be clean again. Fragrant with talc and toilet water.

She had spent ten days in the high plateau searching for mountain gorilla. She thought of the moment she first saw the great silverback male crashing out through the scrub. She had felt a shiver of excitement, but no fear. He had stood watching her for fully five minutes, quite still. Black eyes penetrating hers. She thought inevitably of King Kong and imagined herself Fay Wray. Ridiculous. Ten years fighting for women's rights, writing scathing articles condemning male chauvinism and she goes weak at the knees and starts getting soppy Fay Wray fantasies of abduction and gentle rape by a filthy flea-bitten great ape with yellow tombstone teeth, slobbering Michelin tyre lips and a giant sagging belly swollen with banana shoots. But there *was* something grotesquely beautiful about him. When the female half his size but still enormous, came silently out of the dark undergrowth to join her mate he reached out a massive hand and started to groom her. Monica Burton, smart journalist and sophisticate, suave product of a million generations of evolution, felt the sharp pang of jealousy. It lasted only a moment, then the camera-men came and took their shots and the great beasts, startled, disappeared again into the darkness.

Her husband's hard clean voice cut through her sensuous reverie.

'That was a solid sleep, darling.'

He brought in her breakfast tray. Urbane, civilized, neat and smooth-shaven *homo sapiens* bearing a silver tray. Ugh!

She smiled a warm smile because husbands expect it when they bring their wives breakfast.

She was still naked from the shower. He didn't look at her below shoulder level. But then neither had the giant silverback. She threw on her robe and sat down on the bed.

'Your colleagues from Grub Street have been on the phone.'

Supercilious bastard. He always called it Grub Street even though at other times he seemed quite proud of her profession. It made him feel superior. 'They want a follow-up story. I said you were sleeping.'

He handed her the *Guardian* and kept the *Telegraph* for himself.

She looked at it greedily. She had supplied the original story to the agency but was anxious to see the morning's embellishments.

'They *have* given it a splash.'

'Naturally,' he said. 'It has all the swashbuckling elements that quicken a news editor's pulse in these grey days.'

'You sound rather sour this morning, Charles?'

'I'm sorry, darling. I'm just a trifle bored with idiot reporters trying to hint at a romantic attachment between my wife and her intrepid rescuer.'

She looked at him sharply.

'He was very brave, Charles. But for him I would almost certainly have been killed.'

'Yes, I know,' he said quickly, backing down. 'And believe me, I'm deeply grateful to him.'

He put a hand on her cheek. She softened a little, even though his hand was cold.

'Are you jealous?'

'Of course.' He smiled his gleaming white private dental treatment smile. '*I* should have liked to be the knight in shining armour.'

'Don't be absurd, Charles. That's not a husband's role.'

'Then what is?'

'You guard the keep,' she said, to make him feel protective.

He laughed. 'Should we invite him to dinner?'

'Who?'

'Captain Blair. I gather that's his name.'

She had been thinking of the great ape. Somehow the two had become confused. 'Yes,' she said, trying not to show too much eagerness. 'I was going to do that anyway. I think you'll like him. He's your kind of madman.'

Charles Burton smiled wryly. 'You mean he's *your* kind of madman.'

When Tony Blair left the airline's head office in Regent Street he wandered aimlessly down towards the Haymarket, pushing his way through the jostling crowds of foreign tourists. As a young man he had loved London. Now he hated it. What had once been a distinctively national capital city with an exciting cosmopolitan flavour was now a sleazy Tower of Babel. Germans, Dutch, Americans, Japanese and every third passerby, it seemed, an Arab. Where in God's name had they all come from? He suddenly realized with a jolt that he, and a hundred other airline pilots like him, was partly to blame, for they were the ferrymen. Each plane load of passengers he had landed at Heathrow had been poured down the funnel until the city was overflowing. Over the period of fifteen years he had been flying commercially, Tony Blair had developed an increasing dislike for passengers. Of late he had found it harder and harder to conceal. As captain he was supposed to show his face – in the first-class cabin at least. Share a few meaningless clichés with boring, half-drunk businessmen, pass the time of day with pallid holidaymakers, tripping over their spilling handbaggage and all the time keeping up the company image of a solidly reliable, unflappable gold-braided nanny. There had been times when he could cheerfully have dumped the whole rowdy lot of them at some benighted stopover and flown off without them. It wasn't really the passengers' fault, he supposed. It was airline policy to pour booze down their throats the moment they left the ground and turn every plane into a flying bar. Then tip them, half stewed, out at the other end. But wherever the fault lay, it all added up to the same thing in Blair's mind. He was heartily sick of passengers. So what the hell? – it was time he got out! Left it to the younger men. It wasn't really a job for a flyer any more. What the airlines really needed were highly skilled technicians. Beautifully mannered robots to command the increasingly complex computers that made up a modern flight deck. That's why he had got such a kick out of the odd trip in Mason's clapped-out old Britannia. It wasn't just the chance of earning a few quid on the side. Middleton had known that, he was just trying to hurt him. In a Britannia you could feel the plane under your backside. You were flying. And Blair loved flying. There was no other experience like it in the world.

As he reached the underground car park where he had left his Volvo Sports, he knew what he must do. He no longer gave a damn about the decisions Trans-Africa Airlines were even now making about his future. He would quit the smart, well-heeled world of jumbo jets and the latest impersonal monster, the Tri-star. He would fly cargo. There would be a pretty heavy drop in salary, but so what? No job is worth the money unless you enjoy it.

He drove back to Stanwick feeling a free man.

'So who finally coughed up for the fuel and the landing fees at Cotonou?' Ray Mason asked.

'The people I hauled out of Ximbali,' said Blair. 'They had a whipround, but Mrs Burton coughed up most of it. Her old man cabled some cash through.'

'Quite right, too,' said Mason. 'They got a free ride.'

'The money came through inside an hour,' said Blair pointedly. 'You told me on the phone it would take you twenty-four.'

'I've got problems,' said Mason tersely.

Kim Hayward was on the phone in the traffic office telling an irate caller that Mr Mason wasn't around at the moment. She cupped the phone and said quietly: 'It's the agents for that Ximbali freight. They're doing their nuts!'

'Dubai,' said Mason.

'I'm afraid he's on his way to Dubai at the moment and won't be back for a couple of days,' Kim lied sweetly. She was used to lying on Ray Mason's behalf.

'Why didn't you load it overnight?' Mason asked Blair.

'There was no one around to give customs clearance. It was a damn good job I didn't. I'd never have cleared that tank with ten ton of machinery aboard.'

Mason grunted.

Blair began to get annoyed. 'You were bloody lucky to get your aircraft back in one piece. Don't thank me for it, will you, you miserable old sod.'

'What do you want thanks for?' said Mason. 'You've hit the headlines. You're the hero of the week.'

Blair flared up. The two men stood toe to toe swearing at each other until Kim shouted for them to shut up. She had Mason's bank manager on the phone.

'Tell him I'm in Peking!' said Mason.

'Talking of banks,' Blair shouted, 'where's my money for that flight?'

Mason hadn't paid him yet.

'Come outside a minute, Tony,' Mason said quietly. 'I want to talk to you.'

They left Kim sweet-talking the bank manager and left the Red-Air offices to walk out towards the cargo sheds where no one could hear them.

Mason said he didn't want Kim to know, but things were getting a bit hairy. The company, he said, was suffering from what he called a cash-flow fatigue.

'What are you on about? Kim's sitting there stalling off your creditors. She knows your affairs better than you know them yourself!'

'She's used to that,' Mason said. 'What she doesn't know is that it's for real this time. There's nothing in the piggy bank. I'm going to have to stand her off next week.'

'You're always pleading poverty,' said Blair. 'You do it in your sleep.'

'Notice all the activity around here?' Mason asked.

Blair looked around. Normally there would have been a couple of loaders standing around the sheds waiting to shift cargo. Ground staff out on the tarmac, an engineer working on the plane. Today it was like a desert.

'I'm broke,' said Mason. 'Flat broke!'

'Pass me my violin.'

'You'd better believe it, Tony. That last shipment was my last hope of getting out of trouble. It was cash on the nail and you've left it behind in Ximbali.'

Blair knew Ray Mason of old. Whenever he was in trouble it was someone else's fault. He grabbed him by the arm. 'Listen, mate. You either pay me what you owe me or I'll stick a ticket on that old crate of yours and claim the salvage money!'

Mason glanced around apprehensively. He had heard a car draw up in the approach road outside. He glanced through the side door to see two men get out and head purposefully towards the Red-Air offices. They looked as though they meant business.

'Tony,' he said quietly, 'keep walking.'

He hurried across the apron to the Britannia, Blair after him.

Once inside he closed the hold door on them.

'Bailiffs,' he said curtly.

Blair stared hard at him for a moment. Mason really did look alarmed.

'It's really got to the point where you've got to lock yourself in your own plane?'

Mason nodded.

'So my crew and I risked our necks to get this crate out of Africa and we don't even get paid for it. Is that what you're telling me?'

'That's about it, Tony. I'm sorry.'

'Then maybe you'd *better* take off for Peking. Right now!'

'I can't afford the fuel,' said Mason ruefully.

As Blair drove back to his cottage ten miles from Stanwick airport, he began to have second thoughts about his brave scheme to quit his well-paid job with Trans-Africa. He had fully expected Mason to offer him a permanent crew job with Red-Air. Despite their frequent battles, they were old friends. He had once flown with Mason on the old DC 6s on the Cathay run before Mason started his own company. He'd got so used to Mason crying wolf over the past year that he'd found it hard to believe the man really was in deep financial trouble. Small carriers tended to operate on a 'feast or famine' basis. A few good hauls with full loads on both outer and return legs of the journey and they were flush for a few weeks and could pay off all their debts. But during slack periods, when the plane was either sitting on the ground for days on end, or flying half empty, they juggled around robbing Peter to pay Paul. They were all gamblers in a high-risk business. But one way or another, they always paid their crews. Mostly ex-pilots themselves, they knew this had to be the first priority. You had to trust that crew with the one thing your livelihood depended on – your plane. Welsh on them and the next time they fly out to a pleasant little spot like Nice or Mombasa they could find a dozen technical reasons why the aircraft wasn't fit to fly and they'd have to lay out on the beach for a week. Since a Britannia on the ground was costing the operator around a thousand pounds an hour, any disgruntled pilot had the company by the short hairs.

So, reasoned Blair, Mason must have been telling the truth when he said he was finished. In which case he'd have no choice but to sell up and cash in on the assets. A dozen others had gone the same way over the past couple of years in the cut-throat world of international air freight. Blair could, of course, have applied for a job with one of the larger freight carriers. But not too many of them were still flying turbo-props – the Britannia and the CL 44, the stretched version. Most were now into the big jets, DC 8s or DC 10s, Boeings or the new wide bodies now being adapted for cargo. If he was going to fly the big jets he might as well try and make peace with Trans-Africa and apply for transfer to their freight division. The main attraction of going to Red-Air was Mason's Brit. It was a real plane and over the years he had been sneaking away to fly it as a moonlighter it had become like his favourite armchair. He had once flown Britannias in the RAF and always kept his checks up to date.

As he parked his car in the drive beside his cottage he began to wonder what would happen to Mason's plane. Presumably it would either be stripped down for spares or sold off cheap to some other mug. Some other mug . . . he suddenly had a thought. It was probably daft, but Tony Blair was the kind of man who acted first and thought about things later. He ran into the empty cottage and snatched up the phone. Dialled Red-Air's number.

'Ray, it's Tony. Listen. If you're selling up, how much

do you want for that ramshackle, clapped-out old string-bag of yours?'

'A quarter of a million,' said Mason at the other end.

'I've seen 'em knocking around for a lot less.'

'Not with four good engines, mate.'

'Give me your rock-bottom price, Ray.'

There was silence for a moment, then Mason said, grudgingly, 'If it was cash on the nail I might take two hundred thousand. Who's asking?'

'I am,' said Blair.

He hadn't the slightest idea how he was going to raise it.

2

Blair's cottage was ten miles from the airport. Near enough to get on duty in a hurry, but not so close that he couldn't do a bit of gardening occasionally without having his eardrums shattered. It was actually two nineteenth-century farm cottages joined together, gutted and re-designed to provide three good bedrooms and a fair-sized bathroom on the top floor, two long reception rooms below and a pine-panelled farmhouse-style kitchen. This had been Janet's idea. She was good at interior design and had enjoyed it. Paul had occupied the back bedroom, they took the front. The other one stayed empty. There was only the one child. They had wanted another, but it hadn't happened. Blair sometimes wondered if things might have worked out any differently if it had, but this was now idle speculation. For the past ten years, Tony Blair had lived in the cottage alone. He stayed in the same bedroom and still used the double bed. Apart from the bathroom, the only other room he ever seemed to occupy was the kitchen with its cosy oil-fired Aga stove. He ate there, entertained callers there and, for convenience, had the telephone transferred there. The other rooms just lay and gathered dust.

Not that Tony Blair was always alone. Over the years there had been a succession of young air hostesses spending the odd night there. A few, those with a home-making gleam in their eyes, had sometimes tried to open up the other rooms, tidy, even spring clean. But Blair had learnt to lay down a few rules. The moment a girl started to look as though she was nesting, out she went. He had a local woman in to clean and take his washing to the laundrette. At first she used to cluck away censoriously at the half-empty bottles of nail varnish, the blonde hair choking up the shower drain and the occasional pair of knickers left on the radiator to dry while their owner went off to Majorca on a day charter. But she was used to it by now and seemed to regard the various abandoned items of cosmetics as her legitimate perks. If Blair went for more than a month without a visitor these days, she would even start dropping heavy hints, like, 'Whatever happened to that tall, pretty girl from British Caledonian, you know the one – used to have that gorgeous Chanel scent?'

'She walked out on me after you nicked her nightie,' Blair would say and they'd both laugh conspiratorially.

But Blair spent this particular night alone. He was glad, he had a lot to think about. He was still in great demand by the press who were planning an in-depth story for the Sundays. They'd already sniffed out that he was in trouble with Trans-Africa, and were pressing for statements from the horse's mouth. The 'Hero of Ximbali' grounded for rescuing a group of whites from certain death looked like a good, juicy excuse for opening up the main story again. In loyalty to the airline he had tried his best to head them off, but finally had to hang up on them, to take the phone off the hook for the night and refuse to answer the door-bell.

The following morning he was woken by persistent knocking. But this time it was not the press, but a rather sheepish-looking Captain Middleton. Trans-Africa Airlines had also been considering the problem and had finally come up with what they thought was a reasonable solution.

'If the company publicly accepts that you were moon-lighting,' said Middleton as they discussed it in Blair's kitchen, 'it's a *carte blanche* for any other pilot to do the same and expect to get away with it.'

'So what do you want me to do?' Blair asked.

'Tender your resignation,' Middleton said, looking embarrassed.

'In other words, I'm fired,' said Blair. 'Do I tell the press that?'

He knew he had the airline over a barrel.

'We've already issued a statement to the press,' said Middleton. 'You resigned your position as fleet captain with us *before* you took that flight with Red-Air to Africa. You therefore had our permission to do so.' Blair smiled. The Old Man had worked that one out to get them off the hook.

'And suppose I deny that?' he asked casually. 'Can you produce written evidence?'

'Tony,' said the senior staff captain, more in sorrow than in anger, 'have we ever treated you badly? You got us into this spot, why not help us out. We can come to an arrangement.'

'Golden handshake?'

'If you play it our way, Tony, why not?'

'How much?'

'Ten thousand,' Middleton said tentatively.

'Shove off, Frank,' said Blair. 'I can get twenty for flogging an exclusive to the press.' One of the papers had hinted at it the night before. Providing, of course, it was the full dirt, not a doctored version approved by Trans-Africa Airlines.

'All right,' said Middleton, 'I might be able to swing fifteen for you – as a friend.'

'Make it twenty-five and it's a deal,' said Blair.

'Fifteen's as high as we can go,' said Middleton. 'Stop trying to screw us.'

Blair crossed to the phone and put it back on the hook. Fortune smiled on him. A moment later it started ringing.

'That'll be one of the Sundays,' Blair said, his hand hovering over the instrument. 'What do you want me to tell 'em – Buccaneer Blair fired? That's great publicity for Trans-Africa.'

'All right, you bugger. Twenty-five. But that's your lot!' Middleton shouted.

'It's a deal, Frank,' said Blair.

He had his first £25,000 towards buying Mason's old plane.

The phone call was from Monica Burton, inviting him to dinner.

The tiny Filipino glided to and fro between the main room of the Burtons' elegant penthouse flat and the roof garden. Charles Burton hired Filipinos by the batch from a catering staff agency whenever he was entertaining. He never really knew what sex they were, and didn't care much since he only lusted for people taller than himself. Another Filipino let Captain Blair in. Blair thanked him in Spanish. The Filipino, who was an honours graduate in English literature, merely bowed.

If Monica Burton was surprised to see the smart, close-shaven pilot in hacking jacket and well-creased Daks and relate him to the tough-looking man in crumpled uniform she had last seen at Stanwick airport, Blair was even more amazed to see her. The wild-eyed woman in scrubbed jeans and dirt-stained denim top was now transformed into an elegant beauty in an off-the-shoulder shimmering silk evening dress. He found he could hardly take his eyes off her for the rest of the evening. Charles Burton affected not to notice.

After polite cocktails, the honours graduate announced that dinner was served and they moved on to the roof garden.

Protected from the weather by glass, the garden was paved in Italian marble with a small fountain playing in the centre. They dined from a Florentine table beneath flowering bougainvillaea. From there they could watch the traffic crawl across Westminster Bridge ten storeys below, and see the Thames wind towards Putney. It reminded Blair of the flight deck of a jumbo, so he was rather less impressed than the Burtons' usual guests. But they certainly appeared to be rich.

Charles Burton, it emerged in conversation, was a director of several companies, but seemed casually vague about what they did, or his exact role in them. When Blair was not feasting his eyes on Monica he examined Burton. Hard to tell his exact age, but hovering around the forty mark. Neatly balanced features, but cold grey eyes. Clinical. Resilient, perfectly mannered, but sharp. At first Blair thought he was a typical City man, but there was none of the easy-going confidence of the public-school type. Of short to medium stature, his body was lean and compact. No spare flesh from long boozy lunches. This man was a dynamo and would probably make a ruthless enemy.

At the moment, it was all charm. Burton thanked Blair sincerely, though not profusely, for saving his wife. He commended his bravery and said how he deeply admired initiative which was the foundation stone, in his view, of courage. Monica, Blair noticed, looked slightly embarrassed at the speech and shifted the subject to Blair's immediate future. Having spent the day in Fleet Street she knew that he had been forced to resign from Trans-Africa Airlines.

Blair, according to his bargain with the company, started to give the company's official version, but Monica spared him having to repeat the lie. 'Everyone in Fleet Street knows the real story,' she said. 'Unfortunately no one can print it in case Trans-Africa sues, unless, of course,' she smiled, 'it's under your signature.'

Blair said he had a deal and she did not pursue it. When he had first been invited and discovered that Monica was a journalist, he had suspected she might be trying to steal a march on her colleagues, but she didn't seem to be doing so. Monica explained that while, like any journalist, she would sell a news story if it came her way – as she had done when she had made the call from Cotonou – hard news was not her trade. She was a freelance who concentrated on in-depth material and general interest features.

'And the odd bit of campaign journalism,' added her husband with the faint hint of disapproval in his voice. 'At the moment it's the preservation of the mountain gorilla. Last month it was blue whales.'

'Good for Monica,' said Blair. They were already on first-name terms.

She smiled at him warmly. 'You approve?'

'I respect nature,' Blair said. He'd flown over so much of it in the wild and, like most airmen, was thrilled at the vastness of it, and apprehensive at the cutting down of forests and pollution of the coastlines that was so much more apparent from the vantage point of the air.

Burton turned to his wife. 'What endangered species do you plan to campaign for next, darling?' he asked.

'Male chauvinists,' she said. 'Though as yet they're hardly rare.' Then she switched the subject back to Blair. His future.

'You can hardly be too worried,' she said. 'I imagine a dozen airlines will be only too glad to snap you up after all this publicity.'

Blair explained that, if anything, it would be the opposite. Airlines these days were not interested in daredevil operators. This was an old, romantic wartime image long dead. They expected their fleet captains to be sufficiently safety conscious not to risk a hazardous take-off. Even though he had been flying a cargo plane at the time, it would still count against him.

'So, as a result of saving half a dozen people's lives, you may find yourself unemployable,' said Burton. He seemed genuinely shocked. Blair warmed to him a little. Clearly this man was a gambler himself.

'Let's say it might make a number of airlines think twice,' said Blair.

A few minutes later, under the mellowing influence of a

good claret, Blair found himself telling the Burtons abou his offbeat idea of buying a freight plane of his own.

Charles Burton sat listening, fascinated. Blair realized that, for the first time since he arrived that evening, he had Burton's total attention.

Kim Hayward often worked late. She knew her boss would never get round to paying her any overtime, though he was always promising it, but she didn't mind. She liked the job, and being conscientious by nature, could never leave anything unfinished. Though an attractive girl, at twenty-six she was still single. There had been plenty of opportunities to land a husband. Half a dozen young air crew gallants, tiring of their normal dates with air stewardesses, had cast romantic eyes over her ever since she first arrived at Red-Air. Highly efficient, terribly well organized and apparently always in control of any situation, she seemed to hold out the promise of an ideal wife to young men who tended to confuse efficiency with domesticity. They visualized her sitting patiently at home in an immaculate, well-ordered house, ready to spring into immediate action with a superbly cooked meal the moment they chose to breeze in from Calcutta or Kano, and breeze out again the following morning: having magically changed from a well-oiled kitchen machine into a voluptuous sensualist overnight. But Kim didn't seem terribly interested in *them*. Apart from that, she had her father to look after and he needed a lot of love and attention.

Ray Mason came in from his office, ready to leave.

'Knock it off now, Kim. You've worked late enough.'

'I've got that insurance claim to finish for the freight lost at Ximbali,' she said.

'Who says it's lost? If the fighting dies and it's still intact we may go back for it.'

She looked up at him in surprise.

'How are you going to find a crew to work for nothing, Ray?'

'You know about that?' Mason still treated her as a child at times.

'The flight engineer was on the phone. He's got four kids and a heavy mortgage, Ray. . . .'

He looked down at the floor and muttered, 'Yeah, I was going to pay him a bit on account.'

'What with? You're way over the overdraft limit, that's why the bank manager was ringing yesterday.'

'I've still got a few quid in my personal account,' Mason said.

He took out his cheque book and asked her to draw cash when the bank opened in the morning.

She put the cheque in her handbag, collected her coat, then paused at the door. 'Is it true you're selling up?' she asked quietly.

So she knew. So far he had only told Blair and his own wife, Audrey. But Audrey and Kim were fairly close. Or maybe it was just obvious.

'Sorry, love, I should have told you.'

'But you thought I'd walk out on you like the rest of the staff, is that the reason?'

'You've every right to. You could get a job anywhere. . . .'

'Ray,' she said softly. 'I'll stay as long as you do. And you can pay me when you're flush again.'

'You're a good kid, Kim. But why should you!'

'Because I think you need someone to keep an eye on you for the next few weeks.'

Mason laughed. 'You've got the cheek of the devil, girl. I'm old enough to be your father.'

'My father went bankrupt,' she said.

Mason walked over to her and put his hands on her shoulders affectionately, subconsciously filling the father role in which she had cast him.

'I'm not going bankrupt, love,' he said gently. 'I've got assets. It's just a question of cashing them in for the best price I can get. Then I'm going to pay off everyone I owe down to the last penny.'

Yes, she thought, he was *very* like her father.

One of the Filipinos brought the cheese board. Another silently removed the empty bottle of Château Palmer and replaced it with a Saar white. They were now down to the economics of air freight. Burton was in his element. Money. To him it was the staff of life. It hadn't taken him a moment to realize that this single old plane was capable of generating a cash flow of three and a half million a year if it could be kept in the air for ten hours a day. Blair reminded him that this would depend on full loads for both outward and return legs of each journey, that it would need three crews working in shifts, that old planes need a lot of servicing on the ground and a list of other drawbacks. But Charles Burton now had the bit between his teeth. Like most entrepreneurs in these days of high-interest rates, he was more interested in cash flow than in profit margins. Even a million pounds a year properly invested would yield nearly three times as much in interest charges alone as Mason was asking for the plane itself.

'How long do you think that Britannia can keep flying?' he asked.

'There's six months left on the licence. After that, it has to undergo a thorough CAA test for airworthiness,' said Blair. 'If it fails, it may have to be scrapped or broken up for spares.'

'And if it passes?'

'Then it could go on for another year. It's a gamble, but Brits wear well on the whole.'

'How much did you say he wants for it?'

'Two hundred grand,' said Blair.

'And what do you reckon it's worth?'

'Hard to say. Maybe a bit less.'

'Forgive me for being personal, Blair. But can you raise that yourself?'

Blair said he was going to try.

'Now what about offices, hangar space, air crews,

ground staff? Can you also raise the operating capital?'

Blair had to admit he hadn't really thought too deeply about that yet.

Although he had spent many hours of reveries imagining the joy of being his own boss, taking trips all over the world, heaving cargo from place to place as the fancy took him, he had never seriously considered the tedium of running the ground operation.

'I thought I'd use other operators' facilities,' he said. 'Wet lease the plane to anyone who's short of capacity.'

'Then you're still at their beck and call,' said Burton. He looked disappointed, as though Blair had let down his own image. 'I thought you wanted to build up a business.'

Blair explained that he didn't have an AOC licence to operate as a carrier in his own right, that this took a long time and a pretty substantial cash guarantee.

'I'm not a businessman,' he added, lamely. 'I just like to fly.'

He was aware that Monica was watching him intently. He had been getting eye messages from her all evening which in Blair's experience meant only one thing. She fancied him. What's more, she didn't seem to mind if her husband knew it. Now her steady gaze seemed to imply a challenge. How would he stand up against the hard clinical questioning of her mate? Already Burton was starting to expose him as an impractical dreamer with limited ambitions.

'You could, of course, take over Mason's business lock, stock and barrel,' Burton threw out casually. 'Have you thought of that?'

'He'd want a hell of a lot more than two hundred thousand for the lot,' Blair said.

Burton rose from the table. He explained that he had to leave now as he had to fly to Athens on business.

'Oh? On which flight?' Blair asked, knowing there were no flights to Athens at that time of night.

'I fly on the company plane,' said Burton with a thin

smile. He shook hands with Blair and said how delightful it had been to meet him. Then he kissed his wife lightly on the cheek. As he reached the door he paused.

'If you should decide to buy out Mason's airline, Blair, one of my companies might be interested in putting up finance.'

'On what basis?'

Burton was deliberately vague. 'Some sort of partnership. We'd have to work that out another time. But they wouldn't be interested in simply buying the plane. It would have to be the whole business. Let me know.'

Blair started to walk out with him, presuming it was time to go.

'Please don't feel *you* have to leave,' Burton said. 'And, once again, I am deeply grateful to you. You have fetched me back a very precious cargo.' He smiled at Monica and left.

As soon as he had gone, Monica dismissed the Filipino staff. They had already cleared away the remains of the meal. She was now alone with Blair. Although never slow to take a hint, he felt vaguely uncomfortable. He had the uneasy feeling they had both contrived it this way. After the second brandy she was looking more desirable than ever. She chatted on easily and at her suggestion they moved into the luxurious comfort of the lounge, her hand resting on his arm for a moment as though she was inviting him to seduce her. Blair decided to leave it to her. If she intended him to stay the night, she was quite sophisticated enough to make the running. In these days of liberated women, thought Blair through a warm alcoholic haze, if rape is inevitable, it's a man's duty to lie back and enjoy it. But she made no further moves, and in the back of his mind he could hear an alarm bell that warned him not to mix business with pleasure . . . not yet, anyway.

He got back to his cottage at three in the morning, his mind still fuddled with a delightful mixture of cognac, the delicious scent of Monica Burton and the more astringent smell of her complacent husband's money. There had to be a snag somewhere.

The next morning he started bargaining with Ray Mason. It was only a preliminary skirmish and neither man took the other seriously. Mason said he wanted a half a million for business, licenses and goodwill.

Blair laughed and asked him what bloody goodwill! It was only when Blair hinted that he had a backer that Mason started to prick up his ears.

'If you've got a backer, Tony, fetch him to me.'

Blair laughed. 'No way. He's mine.'

Mason pondered for a few minutes, then proposed his own deal. If Blair could row in some finance, the two of them could form a partnership. Mason would go on running Red-Air, Blair could be his chief pilot with shares in the business. Blair said he'd discuss it with his source of finance. Despite their frequent battles, he was fond of Ray Mason and it didn't seem a bad offer. It meant that Blair could do the flying and Mason could have the headaches.

Kim interrupted them.

'Brian Langley's on the phone,' she said. 'He says he's got a possible buyer.'

Langley worked for Aviation Exchange, a company that specialized in buying and selling anything in the airline industry from spare parts to entire businesses.

Mason had contacted him earlier that day. Mason was delighted. He certainly hadn't expected a response that quickly.

'If you're serious, Tony, you'd better move fast. They're queueing up to buy me out!'

Tony Blair hurried straight on up to London. He knew Charles Burton was still in Athens, but it was a good excuse to see Monica again. This time in daylight.

She looked just as attractive as the night before. If anything, even more sensuous in tight-fitting trousers and shirt with no bra. And she was just as warm and inviting. Tony Blair felt glad he hadn't pushed his luck in the early hours of the morning. He'd reached an age when one-night stands seemed less and less attractive. Too much booze and he tended to drop off to sleep. Better the slow burning fuse of a mounting attraction and the relaxed enjoyment of probing conversation with an intelligent woman.

'New marriage?'

'Two years old.'

'And you're his second wife, so he lets you out on a long leash.'

'Not just a buccaneer, but a marriage counsellor on the side,' she said with an amused smile.

'Just guessing,' he said.

They were seated opposite each other on the white doeskin-covered sofas that formed the centrepiece of the elegant penthouse main lounge. He noticed she used very little make-up, despite the strong winter sun pouring through the plate-glass windows. A touch of lipstick, smear of eye shadow. Blair was pleased. He preferred plain skin.

She noticed his hair was starting to grey around the ears. His neck thicker than it had seemed the night before. A brief image of the great silverback flashed across her mind. Then she thought of the cuddly fat female that snuggled up to him. No, not this primate.

'Either divorced or separated,' she said. Now probing *him*.

'Does it show?'

'There was no tearful wife waiting on the tarmac the day we came back from Ximbali.'

He laughed. 'You've been watching too many war films. Commercial pilots' wives stay at home watching the telly, love.'

She tensed. Her eyes suddenly hard, her voice sharp.

'Don't call me "love", I'm not a barmaid!'

He tried to shrug it off. 'Just a figure of speech. . . .'

She got up and walked across to the window, her back to him.

'If you're going to be patronizing, this relationship is likely to hit heavy weather,' she said coldly.

'What relationship?' He looked across at her back. Long, lithe, beautiful. Blair loved women's backs and had long felt they were grossly underrated as an erogenous zone. A woman's back was cool, firm and alive with deliciously subtle movement beneath the skin.

Somewhere on the outer limits of his sensuous reverie, Monica said, 'Any association with Charles is bound to bring us into frequent contact.'

Blair got up from the sofa and walked towards her.

She turned and their faces were close. The harshness had gone from her voicc. 'And you saved my life. That surely implies some kind of relationship.'

He kissed her. His hand running gently down her spine. 'I think you're using me to make your husband jealous,' he said without rancour.

She made no attempt to deny it.

'Do you mind?'

'Not at all. I enjoy the role. But how seriously do you want me to play it?'

'How badly do you need that plane?' she asked.

It was only after he had left that he remembered his pretext for the visit. He rang her from a callbox to say that Mason wanted half a million for Red-Air – if she happened to be in contact with her husband. She said he phoned her every evening and she would pass on the message. She then added that she didn't expect him back for a couple of days. Blair wasn't sure if it was a simple statement of fact or a heavy hint.

The chauffeur-driven Daimler drove from Heathrow to Stanwick, pausing only to pick up two men from Burton's office in the City. On arrival at the Red-Air office they marched in together carrying bulging briefcases and asked for Mason. Kim hurried into his tiny cubby hole of a private office to warn him. Thinking they were more creditors he was going to slip away out of the back until Kim told him that the shorter of the three men was called Charles Burton and looked like Blair's money. The other two, she thought, looked like well-dressed hoods. Mason came out to meet them. Burton gave him the briefest of handshakes and introduced himself. Mason looked askance at the other two, both dressed in chalk-striped suits, one thin, dark and Jewish, with pebble-thick glasses. The other square and ginger-haired, with cold Glaswegian eyes.

'Mr Cohen and Mr Craig,' Burton said.

'Are they armed?'

'Only with calculators,' said Burton. 'These gentlemen are my accountants. Would it be convenient for them to inspect your books?'

'What, right now?' Mason asked in alarm. 'You might have warned me.'

Burton looked apologetic.

'I'm sorry, I thought Captain Blair had made an appointment for us.'

Mason suspected he was lying, but couldn't prove it. 'I haven't seen Captain Blair this morning, and he hasn't rung – '

Burton cut him short.

'I take it you're still interested in selling your airline?'

Mason said hurriedly that he was, but the books were in a bit of a mess and not very up to date. . . .

'That's quite all right,' Burton said reassuringly. 'These gentlemen are quite used to finding their way around.' The two accountants took this as their cue, started parking their briefcases and opening them.

Mason had the feeling he was being raided. It had happened a couple of times before when the VAT inspectors had descended on him out of the blue. The CAA men also had the habit of pouncing without warning, but somehow he hadn't expected it from a potential buyer. But it was too late now. Mr Cohen and Mr Craig were already spreading out their blank analysis sheets and setting up their calculators like surgeons preparing for an operation. He gave an eye signal for Kim to co-operate and she hurried into the back to get the books and ledgers. He felt he had to keep his end up.

'Did Blair tell you there's another buyer in the market?'

'Yes,' Burton said casually. 'Assuming there are no substantial debts, we may be prepared to match his offer.'

'I'm talking in the region of half a million pounds,' Mason warned.

But Burton didn't bat an eyelid.

'I'll leave Blair to do the negotiating. Would you excuse me, I have another appointment.'

'I'd like to talk to you, Mr Burton . . .' Mason began. He thought if he could get this man on his own he could talk him into the partnership deal. But Burton was already on his way out.

'Some other time, Mr Mason,' he said, and was gone, leaving his accountants to prepare their report. Mason looked at them helplessly and thought of locusts.

They worked silently and efficiently right through the lunch hour. By four in the afternoon they had finished. They re-packed their briefcases, thanked Kim for her co-operation, gave Mason a limp handshake and disappeared into a waiting taxi without another word.

That evening, Burton called Blair on the phone. His voice sounded cold, clinical and tinged with disappointment. He had the auditor's report in front of him, he told the pilot, and frankly he was surprised that none of Mason's creditors had yet filed suit. Red-Air, he said, was in a mess. He was deeply sorry, but it didn't look to him like a going proposition. Blair reminded him that it was Burton himself who had suggested buying it out on the basis of potential turnover as he had been attracted by the cash flow. So what had changed?

'Blair,' said Burton over the phone, 'if I approach the boards of any of my companies they'll ask the same question. If the business has the kind of turnover we suggested, why has Mason gone broke?'

'Because he's not a very good businessman,' Blair said.

'That's the understatement of the year,' Burton said. 'But there's nothing in this audit to suggest the business stood a chance anyway.'

'Even under new management?'

'It would take too long to restore confidence. I'm sorry, old boy, but Red-Air is a leaky bucket. I suggest you start looking around for something else.' He hung up.

Blair put down the receiver and poured himself a stiff whisky. To hell with the man, why had he raised his hopes? Was it the half-million pounds price tag that had frightened him off? Yet Burton knew the asking price before he had sent his accountants in, Monica had contacted him in Athens. At least, she had rung to say she had. Maybe she'd been lying. Or maybe there was another reason that Burton had suddenly gone cold on the deal. Had he found out that Blair had been making advances to his wife while he was abroad? Yet that didn't make sense either. So far it was Monica who was making the running, and Burton gave the impression that he was quite aware of it – even seemed to be encouraging the liaison. Or had he misread all the signals? There seemed to be some game going on and Blair didn't know the rules. He just had a strong suspicion he was being made a fool of. Well, to hell with them both. He had just decided to call an old air-hostess friend of his to come and help him get down the bottle when the phone rang again.

'Tony, I've been talking things over with Monica.' This time Burton's voice had lost its icy tone. 'She's rather upset and feels we've let you down.'

‘Forget it,’ Blair muttered. ‘I was only interested in the plane anyway.’

‘Tony, I’ve been doing a few calculations. If we can get the price right, it might still be worth it.’

‘I thought you said none of your companies would touch it with a barge pole.’

‘They won’t.’ Burton was all sweet reason now. ‘But I’m prepared to take a gamble with my own money if you are.’

‘I can’t raise that kind of money.’

‘I’m talking about two hundred thousand for the lot. Could you raise half?’

‘He’ll never take two hundred grand!’

‘Try him.’

‘But he’s got another bite,’ Blair protested.

‘Just try that figure on him.’ Burton sounded strangely confident, then he changed the subject.

‘We’ve got a little party here tonight. Monica and I would love you to come up to town and join us, if you’re free.’

Blair said he’d think about it. He then rang Mason to put Burton’s offer price of two hundred grand, but wasn’t at all surprised when Mason laughed and told him to get lost. He said the other people interested in Red-Air had promised to make a firm offer in the next twelve hours so why didn’t Blair just forget about it and concentrate on flying.

Blair said he didn’t have anyone to fly with.

‘Are you interested in going back to snatch that freight out of Ximbali for me?’ Mason asked. ‘I just heard the news. That revolution failed. We can get back in.’

Mason the incorrigible! He was like a bloody yoyo. The other day he’d been down and out with the world crashing round his ears. Now with the prospect of some cash coming in from the sale he was talking of putting the Britannia back in the air again. He reckoned he could grab a few thousand before handing over.

'I'll come with you this time, mate. Just me, you and the spanner. But you can have the left-hand seat. All right?'

Blair was tempted. He had an itch to get back in the air again. But he wasn't going to get caught like the last time.

'I'd want the money up front. Cash. Before we leave the tarmac.'

'That's all right, Tony,' Mason said airily. 'The bank's let me have some more cash on the promise of this sale.'

'Suppose your sale falls through, Ray. I'd still like to offer for your plane.'

'Forget your smartarse ideas and your fancy backers. You're an out-of-work pilot, Tony. I'll see you on the tarmac tomorrow morning.' He put down the phone.

The Burtons never did things by halves. It wasn't just any old champagne the hired Filipinos were liberally splashing into the cut-glass Waterford, but Bollinger '69. By the time Blair arrived it was flowing like water before the water rates went up. At first he had been a bit doubtful about coming at all. He felt like a night in with a nice uncomplicated air hostess to share his whisky bottle. But there seemed to be a conspiracy of fate to send all his best birds to far distant places that night. Maybe it was the migration season. Finally he had to admit to himself that he was starting to get hung up on Monica Burton. She had, after all, tried her best to help him. And as he took the lift up to the penthouse he also remembered that he was still warm in the press as the 'Hero of Ximbali'. Might as well cash in on it with a bit of sophisticated and appreciative company.

A six-foot model with a Dresden face and a gown cut down to her navel was the first to greet him as he stepped through the door. She threw her arms round his neck as though she had known him for years, kissed him passionately on the cheek and breathed through a musk haze, 'Darling, where have I seen you before?'

'You tell *me*,' said Blair who had never set eyes on her.

'You're an actor,' she simpered, gazing into his eyes.

'Try again.' He glanced down her cleavage, but all he could see was ribcage.

'I know,' she squealed triumphantly. 'You were in the paper!'

Not bad for a second attempt.

'But I can't quite remember what you *did*.'

Ah well, thought Blair. Such is fame.

'I'm the new striker for Crystal Palace.'

At that point Monica rescued him. The model staggered off to tell her friends there was someone here from Buckingham Palace. Monica was looking as gorgeous as ever in a simple, full-length Indian cotton dress. Blair thought she'd look elegant in anything. She seemed just as warm and genuinely delighted to see him again. As she steered him by the arm towards a passing drinks tray he looked around at the throng of guests. They seemed oddly ill-assorted. There were three or four obvious fashion models, a couple of earnest-looking but nevertheless attractive women whom he later discovered to be women's magazine editors, two black Africans in Nigerian robes with vivacious women in attendance, a couple of hawk-eyed Arabs, flashing dark glances at the models, and a plump swarthy man who could either be a Greek or a Portuguese wine shipper. Standing out like sore thumbs amongst the exotic ethnic mixture was a Royal Navy rear-admiral in uniform and what appeared to be his staff captain. Later he was to discover a couple of Fleet Air Arm officers. Blair wondered what they could all have in common. Presumably a mixture of his friends and her friends, but where on earth did the naval brass fit in? He asked what it was all in aid of, business or pleasure?

'Charles never separates the two,' she said. 'So I usually top a party up with a few friends of mine to avoid being bored to death.' They started to circulate. She introduced him to the models who all seemed to be called Fiona or Sabine and seemed vaguely connected with women's magazines. A features editress dragged him away and demanded to know why there seemed to be very few female airline pilots. She was thinking of commissioning a piece on it. He muttered something about the job requiring a certain physical strength, but she kept quoting Amy Mollison at him. Finally he told her to try Aeroflot and made his escape on the pretext of rescuing one of the models from the Arabs. It turned out to be the Arab who needed rescuing and he promptly pinned Blair in a corner to discuss the declining role of the American dollar in world affairs. Out of the corner of his eye he could see Charles Burton deeply engaged in conversation with the rear-admiral. Burton smiled across at him but made no effort to engage him any further. As Monica was now equally engrossed with a handsome Nigerian, Blair started to wonder why he'd been invited at all, except to make up the numbers. He decided to get drunk and see what the evening might bring.

Mason sat at his desk in his tiny office surrounded by piles of accounts books, statements and final demands. He should have been home two hours before but he had the quarterly VAT returns to make out. Kim had prepared everything but it still needed checking over. Thank God, he thought, he'd soon be shot of all this nonsense. Like most small businessmen he deeply resented being used by the government as an unpaid tax collector, a job for which he was singularly unsuited. Though he knew enough maths to fly and navigate a plane, he found the adding and subtracting of percentages on a whole range of goods and services, some of which were subject to tax, other zero rated, as exhausting as it was burdensome. But it would soon be over. With the money he reckoned to get from the sale, he, Audrey and the kids would take that long summer cruise he had been promising them for years. After that they would sell up the house as well and buy a farmhouse in North Wales. A few acres of land, keep a few cows maybe. Just enough to provide for his family – lead the simple life. Get to know the kids, recapture his own youth by sharing theirs. Any cash left over and he'd buy a double-barrelled shotgun and if any marauding Vatman dared to set foot on his property. . . .

The phone rang. It was Brian Langley from Aviation Exchange. He'd just heard from his client with a firm offer for Red-Air. Could he make an appointment to see Mason in the morning?

'If you're still at the airport, come on round now,' said Mason. He swept aside the books and ledgers from his desk, went to his filing cabinet and took out a whisky bottle and two glasses. There'd be a bit of tough negotiating, Langley was shrewd and had a pretty good idea what the business was worth in the current market. He also had his agency fees to clear, but Mason was an old hand at haggling. He reckoned he held the trump cards, the client was clearly in a hurry to buy. Unlike Burton, he hadn't even asked to see the books. Probably someone desperate to get hold of an existing licence. When Kim came in to say good night she found her boss quietly humming 'Land of Our Fathers'. The Welsh hills were already beckoning.

Burton finally tore himself away from the rear-admiral, gathered up Monica en route and found Blair on the roof garden where he had again been ensnared by the tall model who had greeted him on first arrival.

'Bedtime, sweetie,' he said, patting her on her tiny rump. Obediently she gathered her bag and left. Blair wondered if he hired them by the hour like the Filipinos.

'Tony,' he said apologetically, 'I do hope you didn't think I've been neglecting you, but I had some business to tie up.' He glanced around quickly to make sure the three of them could not be overheard.

'Now, this freight line. I think we should wrap up Red-Air as quickly as possible. I'll have my solicitors draw up a draft contract in the morning, if that's all right with you.'

‘What do you mean, “wrap it up”?’

‘Buy it. Get that plane in the air and earning.’

‘A few hours ago you said it was a dead loss.’

‘So it was, in Mason’s hands,’ Burton said. ‘In yours I expect things to be very different. I shan’t have a lot of time to keep an eye on things myself, but I take it you’d have no objection if Monica was appointed a working director.’

‘Have you thought of asking *me*?’ she asked distantly.

‘Part time, darling. I’m sure you can fit it in.’

She shrugged. Apparently accepting it. Blair glanced first at Monica, then at Burton. Once again he felt he was somehow being made a pawn in a sophisticated husband-and-wife game, but by now was far too drunk to work it out. Was this a genuine conversation, or had it been staged for his benefit? He tried to collect his thoughts together.

‘Now hang on a minute, Burton. We haven’t offered Mason a sensible price yet.’

Charles Burton looked at Blair as though at an innocent child.

‘Yes, we have. The figure I mentioned.’

Ray Mason could hardly believe his ears.

‘Two hundred grand. You’re having me on!’

‘That’s all they reckon it’s worth, Ray. I’m sorry.’

Mason suddenly got suspicious.

‘Who was bidding?’

Brian Langley said he didn’t know for certain. The enquiry had come from their Athens office.

It was then he started putting two and two together.

An hour later, the Burtons’ guests were leaving the penthouse.

The rear-admiral and his staff captain came over to thank their hosts. Then the admiral turned to Blair.

‘Sorry we didn’t get a chance for a chat, Blair. But from

what Charles tells me, you sound just the man for the job.'

Blair looked puzzled. Burton shot the gold braid a quick warning glance.

'What job?'

But the navy was already on its way out. Blair turned to Burton and repeated the question.

'I mentioned that you and I were taking over an airline and you were running it,' Burton said vaguely, then hurried away to see to some parting guests.

Blair turned to Monica.

'What was all that about? What's been going on here this evening?'

'I've no idea, Tony, she said, looking him straight in the eyes. 'Charles never tells me what he's up to till after he's done it. Sometimes I suspect he doesn't even know himself. Like you, he thinks on his feet.'

Blair had had enough.

'You're lying!' he said harshly.

She flushed red.

'I never lie.' She spat out the words, then turned her back on him and walked away. Blair felt it was time to leave.

He got up late the following morning with the worst hangover he could recall for a long time. He couldn't remember how he had got home during the night but had a vague recollection of hitting Mach 1 in his Volvo Sports down the motorway from London. He made a mental note, not for the first time in his life, that whisky and champagne don't mix. Three coffees and two seltzers later he got the car out again and drifted down to Stanwick in third gear, both windows open to clear his head. He needn't have worried about cold air; when he got into Red-Air's traffic office, the atmosphere was positively sub-zero. And the icicles were emanating from Kim Hayward. She could hardly find the grace to return his greeting. He asked where her boss was. She told him curtly that Captain Mason was out on the apron preparing for the return flight to Ximbali. Blair asked her why she hadn't warned him. It was normally her job to warn the crew to be on standby.

'I didn't know you were flying this trip,' she said archly. 'I was told to approach Captain Saunders.'

'Tell Don Saunders I'll do it,' Blair said.

'I don't take instructions from you, Captain Blair,' she snapped. 'I'm not included in the price.' She walked over and started to pound the telex. Blair still didn't know what he was supposed to have done wrong except that this was clearly not his day. He went out on to the apron and found Mason by the fuel bowzer.

'What's all this about calling in Don? I'll fly your right-hand seat,' he said.

Mason scowled at him. 'I don't fancy your company, mate.'

Blair grabbed him by the arm.

'All right, Ray. What am I supposed to have done now? Get it off your chest.'

There was a mixture of anger and contempt on Mason's face.

'You and your smartarse backer set me up with a rigged offer. Don't play the innocent with me!'

In the bitter exchange that followed, Blair was gradually able to fit the pieces together. No wonder Burton had been so confident they could pick up Red-Air at a knockdown price. Having told Mason he would match his best offer, he had set up a straw man – no doubt prearranged during his Athens trip – to encourage Mason to believe there was genuine competition for the business. Aviation Exchange had acted in total innocence but they too had been conned. The effect, as Burton had calculated, was to get Mason to relax. Only the previous day Mason had persuaded his bank manager to extend his overdraft still further on the promise of keen, competitive bidding for his assets. On this basis he had raised the cash for the second trip to Ximbali. Naturally he hadn't bothered to look around for other potential buyers and now it was too late. Burton probably had pulled this trick several times before when taking over companies in trouble, but it was new to Blair. He was furious that he had been kept in the dark and now, in Mason's eyes, was a fellow conspirator. But there was no way he could convince his old friend he had known nothing about it.

But for better or for worse, Tony Blair slowly realized he was now, barring accidents, part owner of Red-Air, and as Mason stormed up the steps into the Britannia, he shouted, 'Where the hell do you think you're going with my aircraft!'

Two hours later, the Britannia nosed its way out on to the main runway at Stanwick. Blair at the controls, Mason in the co-pilot's seat. Somehow or other, on the long trip to Africa, Blair knew he must make his peace with Mason, for both men knew that Mason still held a vital trump card.

As the cargo plane left the runway, a young man walked into the Red-Air offices. He was dark, slim and suntanned. He carried two suitcases with airline baggage tags marked Salisbury–London. He told Kim Hayward he was looking for his father. He had Tony Blair's eyes.

3

Paul Blair had become increasingly nervous on the long flight to England. It had been a wearying trip. From Rhodesia south to Johannesburg to change flight, then the long haul north again across the African continent.

His mother, opposing the trip, had been alternately resentful and tearful at Salisbury airport. But now her son was in his early twenties she knew she could no longer expect to have him with her all the time. Sooner or later he was bound to go and try to find his father. When the *Rhodesia Herald* carried the Ximbali story and Blair's face had been featured on the front page she knew it would act as the trigger. Although Paul had not seen his father since he was twelve years old, he had never forgotten him. Neither had he really accepted the man who had supplanted Tony Blair in his mother's affections – the man she had run away to Rhodesia with to start a new life. At first Paul appeared to accept that their life had changed and would never be the same again. But he had always kept a photograph of his real father in his room and steadily, over the years, had built up a romantic image of him.

Now he would see him face to face, as a grown man, not a child. He was afraid of the confrontation. Afraid his father would either not recognize him at all or disown him.

From Heathrow he made his way down to Stanwick, steeling himself for the meeting, only to find that his father had taken off again, literally a few minutes before, for Africa. He felt totally deflated and miserable. Although the Britannia was due back the following evening, the delay now seemed agonizing. At Kim's recommendation he took a room at the local country inn used by aircrew on stop-over, the Eagle. He spent the next morning writing a long letter to his mother to say he had arrived safely and describing the journey in minute detail. Paul had a passion for detail. In the afternoon he walked around the airport perimeter, glancing nervously up at the skies to see if the Britannia was approaching. When he finally saw it come in its approach run an hour before dusk he hurried back to the Red-Air offices and waited. Kim had been kind but cool. He did not, as yet, know the reason for her coolness and when he tried awkwardly to raise a conversation about his father, she quickly cut it off. She seemed a rather frightening lady. Later he was to discover otherwise, but Paul Blair, unlike his father, had very little experience of women apart from his mother. He was due to grow up very rapidly.

The return trip to Ximbali was uneventful. Although the control tower was now just a burnt-out skeleton and the hastily organized trailer at the end of the runway which was supposed to look after traffic control was little more than a joke it did not really matter as there was virtually no traffic anyway. Blair landed the Brit and he and Mason hastily organized some curious onlookers into a handling team to get the cargo aboard. They found a fuel bowzer that had miraculously escaped being set on fire during the attack and filled up, paying cash to the nearest man who looked vaguely in charge. They slept that night in the plane and took off again at dawn. Since the senior customs official had been shot, they even got away without inspection. This relaxed Mason a little since he had been expecting to have to pay someone a bribe. On the way out he had been morose and resentful. Apart from the necessary technical exchange between pilot and co-pilot, he and Blair had scarcely spoken to each other. Now, as Blair switched over to auto, he felt they should try and get things sorted out. By the time they got back to Stanwick, they had reached an understanding. Charles Burton was not going to like it, but Blair knew that if he was going to run Red-Air he was going to run it his way and make everyone quite clear who was boss. Ray Mason might never entirely trust him again, but at least Blair could now feel he had not let an old friend down.

Neither man saw Paul when they first came into the traffic office with their papers and logs. He rose from his seat in the corner ready to extend a sweating hand, but his father looked right through him. Now Paul's worst fears seemed to be confirmed. In his father's eyes he no longer existed. It was Kim who drew Blair's attention to the fact that he had a visitor from his past. Blair looked at the boy for several moments before he seemed to be able to grasp the fact that this tall, lean, almost fragile-looking young man with deep-set eyes and amber brown translucent skin was, indeed, his own son.

'I'm Paul,' the boy said, screwing up his courage. 'Hullo, Dad.' He hoped it sounded casual.

'What the hell are you doing here?' Blair said. It sounded like an accusation.

Paul felt his cheeks starting to burn.

'I'm . . . sorry if I gave you a shock.'

The next question came hard at him like a bullet.

'Are you alone?'

'Yes.' Paul was now fumbling. 'Yes, quite alone.'

Then the granite face relaxed.

He reached out a heavy hand and crushed Paul's.

From somewhere behind, Paul heard Mason ask his father if he'd like the privacy of his office. Blair muttered his thanks, grabbed his son by the arm and led him out. When they were alone, Blair seemed to relax a little but there was a cautious suspicion still in his voice.

'Is this a holiday?'

'I'm not really sure, yet,' Paul said.

'Then what prompted the trip?'

Paul said that he'd always wanted to come to England as soon as he had the money for the fare, that he regarded it as his home and that while he was here he thought he'd like to look up his father. It sounded lame, so he added that he'd read about his father in the paper. This seemed to satisfy Blair as a legitimate reason, at least for the moment.

'We were very proud of you,' he added, then realized straight away that it was a mistake to use the plural.

'We?'

'Mother and I,' the boy stuttered.

Blair nodded silently and still held his son in a cold penetrating gaze.

'Did you come because you wanted to, or because your mother sent you?'

'I came because I wanted to see you again, Dad,' the boy said quietly. 'My mother was against it.'

He didn't know whether his father believed him or not, but he appeared to be satisfied, for after a few more questions he asked, 'Where are you staying?'

'At the pub in the village.'

Blair seemed to make up his mind.

'Check out. Bring your bags over here. I've got an hour's work to do. When I'm through I'll take you back to my place.'

Paul protested that he didn't want to impose on his father, but Blair cut him short.

'I've got the cottage still. The one you were brought up in. There's a lot of room and only me in it. You're welcome to a bed.'

'You're quite sure about that, Dad . . . '

His father smiled for the first time.

'Look, Paul. I didn't expect you, and you happen to have arrived at one hell of an awkward time, but now you're here, we might as well get to know each other again.'

'I'd like that,' Paul said quietly. He could feel the tears prickling the corners of his eyes and turned quickly to conceal them.

As he left his father called.

'If we don't get on, I'll sling you out. All right?'

Paul smiled back and hurried out, a desperate sense of relief in his mind. The first confrontation was over and his father had turned out to be all that he had thought him to be during the long, painful period of growing up in a distant land. Tough, stern, but at heart a kind man. They would get on. He knew they would.

Blair stared down at Mason's desk for some time after his son had left, wrapped in thought. It had been a shock seeing the memory of a child turned suddenly into the reality of a man without the slow process of the intervening years.

In that first moment he had known him to be his son, yet he had not known him. He had his mother's build, his mother's hair, his mother's self-effacing smile. For a moment he had the curious feeling he was looking at Janet again and had felt his whole body stiffen. But the eyes were his own and so long as he had held them in his own gaze he could almost believe he was staring at himself through a deep mist of years. A part of his past had suddenly caught up on him long after he had thought it dead and buried. Yet he had always known it must happen some time. He knew there would be some awkward questions. Some painful memories. He hoped there would be no bitterness, but he knew that it must be just as difficult for the boy himself and found himself admiring his son's screwed-up courage. As he tried to concentrate on making out his voyage report he found his thoughts straying into fragments of painful conversation with Janet. He must try to remember that his son was an individual in his own right and not a part of his shattered marriage.

It was certainly a hell of a time to be faced with the past when his own future was suddenly in the balance. Why did it all have to happen at once? Perhaps it was an omen, but whether for good or bad he had no way of telling.

Charles Burton was never idle, even in his sleep, for he had the mind of a puppet master. All the strings had to be kept taut, perfectly controlled. Neglect them for one moment and they would become hopelessly tangled. At the moment, sorting out Red-Air was the first priority. From the moment Blair had first mentioned air freight and its potential for generating cash he had been determined to get hold of it, providing it could be bought cheap. Over the years he had developed a keen insight into the calibre of his fellow men. Like many of the most successful entrepreneurs, he had an almost feminine intuition about people. He knew Blair had guts because he had shown it by his actions. He knew he was impulsive, stubborn if pushed but essentially trustworthy. A man naïve enough to consider honesty a virtue and proud enough to succeed when challenged directly. He also knew that his wife wanted an affair with him. It seemed a propitious combination of circumstances. It meant that in the event of a clash he would have a personal hold on the man. He was arrogant enough to believe this situation could be controlled.

Burton's reaction to Mason was equally succinct. The man was a failure, he had no time for him. More than that, since Burton believed that failure was infectious, he had to be got rid of. Normally that would have been easy enough for a man of his financial talent. All he had to do was to buy up everything he owned and show the man the door. But there was a fly in the ointment. Mason's licence to carry freight issued by the Civil Aviation Authority was not transferable. Normally, a carrier like Red-Air would be bought up by another carrier in the same line of business. They would not need Mason's licence because they would be operating under their own. But Burton was an outsider, and although Blair had been in the business all his working life as a pilot, he had no cargo experience except as a moonlighter. Blair had warned Burton that this would create difficulties, but Burton had passed it off. He felt he could impress the CAA with his experience as a businessman and financial status. But when he called to see the CAA Inspectorate he found he was up against a much tougher body than he had imagined. While they welcomed the news that Red-Air was to have a new injection of capital, they were not prepared to issue a new licence to people without direct experience in the field until they had proved they would maintain the authority's high safety standards. Burton complained that this was catch 22. They couldn't trade without a licence and couldn't get a licence until they had proved themselves as traders. But the authority was adamant. If the new management wanted to operate immediately, it would have to do so under Mason's existing licence and this meant retaining Mason with the company.

Mason, of course, had known this from the beginning. This was his trump card. He had laid it on the line to Tony Blair on the trip back from Ximbali. If they wanted to get that plane off the ground they would have to take him in with them. Since his dream of retiring with a quarter of a million had now been frustrated by Burton's sharp practice, they would now pay the penalty. They were stuck with Mason and in return he wanted a fair slice of the business and it was up to Blair to make sure he got it. This was, in fact, the agreement the two men had reached before they landed again at Stanwick. An elaborate game of chess for control of the new company had now begun.

As soon as Burton heard that the two pilots were back, he arranged a dinner that evening for the four of them – himself, Blair, Monica and Mason. It was agreed that they were to meet at the Eagle which boasted a fine dining room and a good chef. He then fixed a meeting an hour before the dinner at which Mason was not invited. He told Blair there were a few problems to sort out beforehand. Blair only had time to run his son to the cottage and drop him there before rushing off again to meet Burton and Monica in the Eagle bar.

Burton presented his plan for the new company structure. Tony Blair would be managing director, he, Burton, would be chairman of the board of directors. Monica would also act as a director and sit on the board. She would also be concerned with the day-to-day running of the operation on a part-time basis and a suitable title would be found for her. Since, he added, three directors were not really sufficient to run a company – one absentee would render it ineffective, and four might produce voting deadlock, he would propose that two additional directors be appointed to make a total of five.

He had it all worked out, Blair thought. But he'd deliberately left someone out. 'Where does Ray Mason fit into the picture?'

'We are apparently obliged to include him for the time being,' said Burton coldly. 'I suggest he be put in charge of traffic control or something. I'll leave that to you, Tony.'

'He must also be a director.' Blair had promised him that.

'Why?' Burton asked.

'Because he's the licence holder and we can't move that plane an inch off the tarmac without his permission,' Blair said. Surely Burton had got the message.

'He will be engaged by the company as an employee and do what he's told,' snapped Burton. 'I don't want that man on the board.'

Monica glanced towards Blair to see how he would stand up to her husband.

Once again he felt he was being called.

'Well, I do,' Blair snapped back. 'There are two directorships going spare, and as your new managing director, I want Mason to have one of them. Anything else would be humiliating.'

It was now Burton's turn to be called. He stared Tony Blair out for a moment, then turned to Monica.

'What's your opinion, darling?'

'I was wondering when I was going to be asked,' she said tartly. 'As it happens, I agree with Tony. Mason is, after all, the only one of us who knows how to run the business.'

'Badly,' Burton interjected.

'But better than complete novices. I also think it would be dangerous to have a man who holds the power to stop the whole operation treated as a mere employee. He'll resent it and could cause endless trouble.'

Blair nodded vigorously. A sensible approach. He was glad she was around. But she hadn't finished yet.

'But I have no intention of sitting on a board that is male dominated. I want another woman on the board. I suggest the fourth and fifth directors be Mason and Kim Hayward.'

Blair nodded his assent.

Burton suddenly became democratic, a role that ill suited him.

'Very well then,' he smiled thinly in defeat. 'I am out-voted. We have a board of directors.'

And Blair felt he had an ally. It was obvious that Burton, when faced with his determined wife, was prepared to give in to her. Life should be interesting.

Mason then joined them for dinner, and found himself presented with a *fait accompli.* He accepted his appointment as a director as his right, then immediately demanded to know what his share allocation would be. Burton practically choked on his turtle soup. The sheer cheek of the man.

'Nothing,' he said angrily. 'Your investment in this company is a pile of bad debts we shall have to pay off. You're damn lucky to be on the board at all!'

'I want twenty-five per cent of the shares, mate,' said Mason. 'If you don't like it, you can lump it.'

He called for the wine list, then ordered a beer.

'There are no shares left,' Burton said when he had recovered from his outrage. 'They are all allocated between the investors, myself, my wife and Captain Blair. He looked to Blair for support.

Blair was caught napping. He had vaguely assumed that he and the Burtons would have fifty per cent of the shares each, but hadn't thought too deeply about it.

'We'll have to sort that out,' he said, hoping it wouldn't be too soon since apart from the golden handshake from Trans-Africa he hadn't had a chance to try and raise the rest of the purchase money yet.

'You'd better sort it out right now,' Mason said. 'I want to know who's getting the controlling interest.'

'Does that matter at this stage, Ray?'

Burton said sharply that it was none of Mason's business, but Mason ignored him and went on talking to Blair as though the other two weren't present.

'Of course it matters, you berk. You can stack a board of directors any way you like, but if you let the Burtons have more than fifty per cent of the shares between them, they can call a shareholders' meeting, dismiss the board and flog the assets before you know what's hit you.'

Burton intervened before Blair could catch his breath.

'The stock in any company must reflect the investment, as you know perfectly well, Mason. We are providing half the purchase money and the initial working capital. That entitles us to a fifty-one per cent stockholding at least.'

Mason turned to Blair in triumph.

'What did I tell you, Tony. They've got you by the short and curly.'

Blair knew he was starting to get out of his depth. He wasn't even sure which side anyone was on any more. This was now developing into a battle between Mason and Burton over his head. But once again it was Monica who stepped in to cool it down.

'I suggest that no one has a controlling interest,' she said. 'But I do think that Tony Blair should be the largest shareholder. It was his idea in the first place and he will be in effective charge.'

Once again her husband seemed to defer to her.

'Very well,' he said after a moment's thought. 'I propose that Tony holds forty per cent of the shares, Monica and I hold twenty-five per cent each and the other ten should be divided between the other two directors.'

Mason tried to interject but Burton talked over him.

'That is a very generous offer on our part. We have effectively ceded control. I now intend to take a vote on that.'

Monica assented immediately. It was now up to Blair. It sounded all right to him. He was getting the lion's share.

'I agree,' he said, averting his eyes from Mason.

Mason protested volubly. Half the other customers in the restaurant stopped eating to turn round and look at him. No way, he said, was he going to be content with five bloody per cent, and who the hell was the other director anyway? No one had told him yet.

'Kim Hayward,' said Monica.

'She's my bloody assistant! I trained her. When she came to me she was only a typist.'

'Does that make her a second-class citizen?' said Monica icily.

Mason stormed out of the restaurant, his meal half finished. He had been robbed, insulted. He had expected that from Burton, but not from Blair. He had still regarded Tony Blair as a friend. He had saved him from losing control of the company by pinning Burton down over the fifty-one per cent holding. In return, the bastard had given him the Judas kiss when that smooth bitch handed him a big slice of the cake. Then, as a final humiliation, elevated his own secretary with an equal share on the board.

He stopped off at his favourite pub on the way home to drown his sorrows. When he got home, stoned out of his mind, his wife Audrey was waiting up for him.

'I was gypped,' he said. 'Conned bloody rotten.'

'You're always getting conned,' said Audrey indignantly. 'I don't know why you put up with it.'

Paul had also stayed up, waiting for his father. When Blair discovered he hadn't eaten, he insisted on preparing a steak for him.

'I'm a frying-pan man,' he said, as he slapped the bit of fillet he'd been saving for himself into a buttered pan. 'You get that way when you live on your own.'

Paul laughed and said he didn't mind.

'What do you drink? Or *do* you drink, son?'

Paul said he wasn't fussy.

'I expect a son of mine to be more positive than that,' Blair said. 'What did you miss most out there in Rhodesia during the sanctions?'

Paul smiled and said, 'A decent French wine.'

Blair selected his best bottle of claret from the rack and then settled down to share it while the steak fried. Blair was pleased with the evening's work. A lot had been settled. He was now firmly in control of Red-Air, thanks largely to Monica's interventions. Mason had felt wronged, but he always did. He'd get over it. When he did, he'd realize he hadn't come out of it too badly. In fact, everything seemed to have turned out very fairly in Blair's opinion. The only thing that troubled him slightly was why Burton had given up financial control so easily. Could it be just to please his wife? If so, she must have a very strong hold over him. Blair now felt mean for suspecting the two of them had somehow been working together. He looked forward more and more to working alongside this fascinating lady on a day-to-day basis. He smiled to himself, forgetting that Paul was there.

'Good meeting, Dad?'

'Yes,' said Blair. 'I think so.' He then realized that Paul didn't have a clue yet as to what was happening. Over the steak he told him about the developments. The boy seemed genuinely excited. Up till then he had merely thought of his father as an ordinary airline pilot, not as the owner of an airline.

Blair laughed. 'It's one knocked-out old aircraft, that's all,' he said, 'and I don't even half own it yet. I still have to raise the cash.'

That was a sobering thought. Now he'd have to do it in a hurry. He reckoned he could sell the cottage, there was no mortgage on it. Raise an immediate bank loan on the basis of the sale and look around for a flat to rent. He explained this to Paul. He felt he had to warn him that he wouldn't be staying in the cottage too long. But Paul didn't seem worried. He was so obviously delighted to be sitting down again in his old home talking to his father that if Blair had told him they were both going to sleep in a ditch from there on he wouldn't have minded.

After a while, Blair realized that the whole conversation had been centred around him and his activities. He still knew nothing at all about his son's affairs. He broached the subject delicately.

'Where exactly were you living?' He knew that his ex-wife and her boyfriend had a farm but that was years ago. There had been no contact since.

'Alan sold that, during the fighting. It was close to the border.'

'That must have been a bit hairy.'

Paul shrugged. 'I was in the army at the time. I think that's why Alan finally decided to get out and move to Salisbury. There was no one to protect Mother if he had to go out anywhere.'

'You still call him Alan,' Blair asked tentatively.

'What should I call him?'

'Not "Dad"?'

'I never accepted him in that role.'

'You had every right to, and he had every right to expect it,' Blair said.

'I make my own judgements.' Paul looked shyly at his father and laughed. 'I dare say I inherit that from you.'

'That's a funny word to choose, judgements.'

The boy looked away. 'I mean . . . I don't hold you to

blame for the separation. It was Mother who left *you*, not the other way round.'

Blair began to feel anxious at the boy's unswerving sense of loyalty and felt he had to adjust the balance.

'It takes two to separate, Paul. Don't blame your mother for everything that happened. I was away a lot . . . she needed company. . . .'

'I'm not laying any blame,' the boy said hastily. But clearly he was.

'Fine,' said his father. 'Let's leave it there, shall we.'

It was getting late. They could continue this some other time.

Paul slept in his old room that night and felt the memories of childhood flooding back. It seemed much smaller than he remembered it, the ceiling lower, the walls closed in. But it had remained indelibly *his* room. His bed, his bookshelves that still contained his books. His little desk where he had spent endless hours poring over his homework, the old-fashioned Victorian fireplace where he had so often quickly stubbed out his first illicit cigarettes on hearing his mother's footfalls coming up the stairs. Over the years someone, presumably spring cleaning, had taken down the posters from the walls, but he found them rolled up in the bottom of the wardrobe. The wooden hangers were empty now and he wondered what had happened to his old school duffel coat that had seemed an unnecessary item to take with him to sun-soaked Africa. He supposed it had gone to a jumble sale. His old toys were missing, too, but he had hardly expected to find them. Then he remembered something. He reached to the top of the wardrobe and there, hidden behind the architrave, buried deep in dust, was the kukri – the curved, broad-bladed Gurkha sword his father had brought back from India for his tenth birthday. He remembered standing quietly at the top of the stairs listening to the row it had caused between his parents. His mother had said it was far too dangerous a weapon for a boy of his age and accused his father of reckless irresponsibility. The argument had soon spread out into other, more personal areas. Accusations and resentments that must have been building up for some time between the two but to Paul were as alarming as they seemed irrelevant.

All he knew was that his treasured birthday present was at the heart of it all, or seemed to be. He had crept back to his room when he found he could not bear to listen any longer, his eyes full of tears. Some time later he heard the front door slam and heard his father's car start up and drive away. Later still his mother had come up to his room. She seemed completely in control of herself again, though her eyes were still red at the corners. She told him that his father had made a mistake. The kukri was for an older boy, a cousin of his. But Daddy had left some money for him to buy whatever he wanted instead. He took the money, knowing it had come from her handbag, and handed her back the sword in silence. She had tried to cuddle him, but he remained stiff and tense. He found the sword the next day at the bottom of the dustbin, retrieved it and hid it away from her sight at the top of the wardrobe. His father did not come back again for another ten days. His mother told him he was in Malaya.

Twelve years later, Paul Blair, now twenty-two years old, recovered his tenth birthday present, polished the blade till he could see his face in it and resolved to keep it for the rest of his life.

He slept peacefully that night and rose early. As soon as he was dressed he went out to the back of the cottage. It was here that Paul suffered his first tinge of disappointment. The long, neat garden he remembered had disappeared. In its place was a wild, overgrown scrub. The fruit trees that had once seemed so strong, fecund and laden with red apples and fat pears were now coarse barked and shrivelled like old men. On the lower branch of the cherry tree were two circular ridges, wounds cut deep into the flesh like long-healed circumcision scars. The branch was now dead, strangled by the two wire loops that had once supported his swing. Beyond the tiny orchard, buried deep in nettles, he found some strands of rust-eaten chicken wire.

His father walked quietly up beside him.

'No chickens any more.'

'No one to feed them while I was away flying.'

Paul nodded silently and walked on to the far end of the garden where it bled into cornfields.

'There used to be a summer house.'

'Yes . . .' His father smiled ruefully. 'Finished up as firewood, I'm afraid.'

'That was my radio shack,' Paul said.

'Oh yes, so it was . . .'

'I used to send you messages . . . well, pretend to send you messages. To all sorts of exotic places . . . like Singapore . . . Delhi . . . Bangkok . . . wherever I thought you were.'

He did not look at his father, only at the growth-tangled ground, and his voice sounded far away.

'What sort of messages?'

'Oh, things about school . . . or that my guinea pig had died . . . nothing very important.'

Blair knew that to a child that age, who had always been sensitive, these pretend messages had been desperately important. The boy had been lonely, these had been his cries for help to a father who was always somewhere else; who would arrive home for a day or two, distribute presents, then disappear. At that time he had been on the Far East run, Hong Kong, down to Singapore or Kuala Lumpur, on down to Port Moresby or Darwin, then back up the Malay Straits. He was often away for two or three weeks at a time.

It was soon after this period that his marriage had broken up. Although Blair stoutly maintained to himself this was not the main reason why his wife had taken their son and left him, he knew in the back of his mind it was a strong contributory factor. He suddenly felt a pang of guilt about the radio shack, and felt he must explain.

'It fell down, one February, in a gale. Didn't seem worth building it again.'

'So you burnt it.' Though he said it quietly and without accusation, there was a touch of bitterness and loss in Paul's voice.

Blair said gently, 'Perhaps you'd be happier walking around on your own.'

He went back into the house. When Paul joined him a few minutes later he seemed bright, cheerful and full of enthusiasm again, his nostalgia had disappeared.

Blair said he had a busy day. He was going to the house agents to put the cottage on the market, then to see his bank manager to raise a loan against the future sale. Paul asked if he could come along, too, adding deferentially that he might be able to help.

'Are you any good at figures, son?' Blair asked with a laugh.

'Reasonably.'

Blair asked him to work out the interest payments on a £60,000 loan over a period of two months. This was the amount he hoped to be able to raise on the house. Paul gave him the answer in seconds. He also gave the figures for three and six months without apparently pausing for thought.

'Not bad,' said Blair admiringly. 'What do you do for a living, Paul?'

So far he hadn't got round to asking.

'I'm an accountant,' said his son shyly.

Mason didn't show up in the office that morning. Kim began to get worried and was in no mood to be friendly when Monica arrived to offer her a seat on the board of Red-Air and five per cent of the stock. She reacted with deep suspicion, particularly when she heard that it was

Burton's proposal.

'What about Captain Mason?' she asked curtly.

'He'll also be on the board with the same equity,' said Monica.

'Has he agreed?'

'Not yet.'

'Then if you don't mind,' Kim told her, 'I'll wait till I've discussed it with him.'

Monica looked at her sharply.

'Can't you make up your own mind?' The hardest part of sticking up for women's rights, she discovered, was persuading other women to take advantage of them.

'How did Captain Mason react to the proposal?' Kim asked cautiously.

Oh, for God's sake, Monica thought. The stupid girl can't take a step without her boss's approval. Maybe she'd made a mistake suggesting her.

'Do you really want to know?'

'Yes.'

'He was horrified. He said you were just his bloody typist. Now how does that grab you?'

'You could be mixing it, Mrs Burton,' Kim said coldly.

'I could, but you know damn well I'm not.'

She did know. It sounded just like a typical Mason remark. But it didn't seem to upset her. Her mind was already racing ahead.

'How would that affect the voting?'

'We'd all have one vote, irrespective of the equity.'

'So a combination of Mason, Blair and I could always defeat you two on a motion, Mrs Burton.'

'Theoretically,' Monica said.

'Your husband's a shrewd man. Why would he risk that?'

Monica was relieved. Kim *was* a bright girl after all. But she didn't have an answer.

'Frankly, I don't know.'

'Who do you think you're kidding, Mrs Burton. You're his wife, you *must* know.' Bright, but old-fashioned. As

Kim leant forward to emphasize her point, Monica noticed a gold crucifix round her neck. That would explain a lot.

'My name's Monica,' she said. 'Now, are you interested or not?'

'I'll let you know, Mrs Burton,' she said.

Kim finally tracked Mason down at lunchtime in the Eagle bar. He'd obviously been at it heavily since opening time.

She challenged him brusquely. 'Where have you been?'

'You're starting to sound like my wife,' he said. Then shouted to the barman to set him up another pint and an orange juice for the young lady since she was under age. But sarcasm wasn't going to get him anywhere. Kim sat down firmly opposite him, ordered a gin and tonic and prepared to sort him out.

But he was ahead of her.

'You're about to tell me that Lady Bountiful has just offered you a bribe and like a good little Catholic girl you're going to take it and confess afterwards. Right?'

'I don't take bribes, Ray, and you know it.' She was finding it hard to control her temper.

'Then learn, my lovely. The world is wickeder than you think, and despite what they taught you in that convent school, the meek only inherit the earth when every other bastard's looted it.'

She gave him a scornful look.

'Are you going to sit here all day feeling sorry for yourself? Why can't you behave with a little dignity!'

That hurt him and she knew it. He glowered at her. 'Don't you bloody lecture me, girl,' he said. 'They cheat me out of my business, and now, because they suddenly discover they can't carry on without me, I'm to be treated like something the cat dragged in! Where's the dignity in that?'

The barman brought the drinks, which gave them both a chance to cool down. She tried pleading with him.

'Ray, you'll still be a director . . . '

'Big deal . . .'

'And I'll be sitting there with you. Frankly, it's better than I expected,' she said.

'Be thankful for small mercies, eh? Is that what you're saying?'

'No,' she said. 'Just swallow your pride for the moment and think ahead a bit. How long do you think this little honeymoon between the Burtons and Tony Blair is going to last?'

Mason shrugged.

'So long as he fancies he can climb into bed with her, I suppose.'

Kim laughed. She knew Tony Blair of old.

'I think you'll find it's the other way round. He's vain enough to expect the woman to do the running. But let's suppose it gets serious, how long do you think Burton's going to put up with it?'

Mason said he didn't know, Burton was a sharp bugger.

'Sharp enough to protect his property if he thinks there's any real danger of losing it,' she said. 'And he's the kind of man who treats a wife as a piece of property. If those two really start going strong he'll have her out of here before she's had time to pull her knickers up.'

Mason laughed out loud. For all her religious upbringing, Kim could be deliciously crude at times. It was one of the reasons they got on so well.

'And when that happens,' she continued, 'you and I can start running things our way.'

'There'll still be Burton himself. And Tony. . . .'

'Would you stay bosom pals with a man who was cuckolding you? They'll be at daggers drawn. The next thing, Burton'll be trying to get rid of Tony Blair. Before you know where you are you'll have your old airline back.' She gave him a knowing smile. 'If you play it clever.'

Mason chewed it over for a few moments. Although Kim had now been with him for five years she never lost her capacity to surprise him. There were times when he couldn't quite work her out. She was efficient enough to get a personal assistant's job in any smart office she cared to choose, and at a higher salary. Yet she seemed content to stay working with him in his shabby little Portakabin. Most of the time she would defer to his judgement even when she thought he was wrong. Her strict Catholic upbringing, he supposed – always let the man think he's in charge for fear of damaging his virility. But she had a shrewd head on her pretty shoulders and could usually see a dozen moves ahead of him. Feminine guile, he imagined, but at the moment he thanked his lucky stars she was using it on his behalf. But then she always did. She was always watching and protecting him.

'I was never much good at plotting out moves,' he admitted finally.

'Then leave it to me, Ray.'

He smiled. 'All right, brighteyes. I'll play it your way. You've got yourself a directorship.'

She didn't even remind him it was not his to give.

As she left the bar he found himself wishing he and Audrey had Kim as a daughter – they had only sons. She would be a very dutiful daughter. Kind, loving, generous and loyal.

He was right on the first three counts. He was in for a shock on the fourth.

It was a day to prove that the oldest are not always the wisest. Tony Blair found his son not merely helpful, but invaluable. He had arranged for an estate agent to handle the sale of the cottage in a quick auction. Paul had insisted they put a reserve on the property because he knew the bank would ask about it, to make sure it covered the loan. At the solicitors, it was Paul who had talked conveyancing jargon and got Blair's sleepy lawyer to shift his backside. When they got to the bank, Blair was only too glad to let his son chat away to the manager about loan repayments, interest scales and collateral. The bank manager had asked to see an audit of Red-Air's accounts before he would agree to finalize the loan arrangements, but once again Paul came to the rescue. As a newly chartered accountant, he promised to provide it within twenty-four hours.

They got back to the cottage that evening tired and happy. It had been a busy and successful day. Blair looked forward to taking his son out to dinner at the best restaurant he could find, but as they got inside the door the phone started ringing. It was Burton. He had to see Blair right away. It was urgent. With Charles Burton, everything was urgent. Blair would have cried off, but Paul insisted he was quite happy on his own and declined his father's offer to take him along. He said he had letters to write.

Blair drove up to London. They were to meet at the Chelsea Grille.

'How soon can we get that plane in the air?'

Burton never believed in small talk before a meal. He was away like a greyhound from a trap before they'd even unfolded their napkins. Monica joined them at the table.

'The sooner the better for my liking,' Blair said.

'Good. One of my companies needs some freight shipped out to the Middle East as quickly as possible. Eighty tons gross weight. How many trips do we need?'

'It's cargo weight against fuel weight. Whereabouts in the Middle East?'

'Abu Dhabi.'

Blair made a quick calculation. The longer the distance in one hop the more the fuel. The greater the amount of fuel, the less the cargo.

'Between five and six loads. Depends what it is.'

'Does that affect the calculation?'

'It would if it was eighty ton of ping-pong balls,' Blair said. 'It's also weight against bulk.'

'Scientific equipment,' Burton said vaguely. 'All crated.'

'You'll have to be more precise than that.'

Every item of freight had to be listed on the manifest for customs clearance, he explained, though he was sure Burton would know that.

Burton lowered his voice as though fearing the hovering waiter was a spy for his competitors.

'This has to be kept confidential at the moment, Tony, for commercial reasons. We have obtained this order in the teeth of some fairly stiff competition.'

'If I'm your managing director, you're going to have to start trusting me,' said Blair.

'It's a consignment of ex-service equipment,' he said at length. 'In this case from the Fleet Air Arm. We have found a customer for it overseas.'

So that explained the presence of the naval types at the Burtons' party, thought Blair. He was immediately suspicious.

'Are we talking about arms?'

'Not in the strict sense,' Burton said quietly. 'Range-finding equipment, gun sights, electronic back-up stuff.'

Monica looked up at her husband in surprise.

'That's not scientific equipment, Charles,' she said sharply.

Again Blair found himself wondering whether Monica had really been kept in ignorance; if not, it was a good act. She looked genuinely shocked.

'I suppose one could say it's intended for scientific warfare,' Burton conceded. 'I really don't know what use it will be put to.'

'It counts as arms,' Blair said bluntly. 'That means you'll have overflight problems.'

He explained that many European countries were very apprehensive about arms being flown over their territories, even at 25,000 feet. Austria, for example, refused it altogether and France could be very sticky. In Eastern Europe there'd be a couple of Migs on your tail forcing you to land and if you chose a southern route and happened to cross Libyan air space, they'd just as likely shoot you down in flames.

'That's why it should be referred to in the manifest as "scientific",' Burton said. 'There's no reason for any country you overfly to be any the wiser.'

'No way,' Blair said flatly. He knew freight captains who'd been caught out before on that one. Usually it was called 'agricultural equipment'. But practically every country in the world was wise to that dodge by now, particularly in the Middle East. A captain could have his licence taken away for accepting a load under a false manifest. Blair wasn't going to risk that.

'So you're not such a buccaneer, after all,' Burton taunted.

Blair suddenly remembered the remark the admiral had made to him at Burton's party: 'just the man for the job'.

He was aware that Monica was watching to see how he would react.

'I'm not such a bloody fool as to carry illegal arms shipments,' he said angrily.

'Who said it was illegal?' Burton asked indignantly. 'Billions of dollars' worth of ex-service equipment is sold world wide every year. Planes, tanks, rockets, you name it. It's a perfectly legal trade.'

'It's a very bloody trade,' said Monica. For once he ignored her.

'If it's over the counter, why isn't the government handling it?' Blair asked.

Normally such a sale would have been handled through a quasi government agency called the British Defence Sales Organization.

'Because it's only a bin end sale,' Burton said. 'Too small for the BDSO to bother with. I have convinced the navy we can do the job more quickly and efficiently.' He looked hard at Blair, daring him to challenge the statement, then added: 'There's enough money in these shipments to repay the entire purchase price for Red-Air. Since it is your money as well as mine at risk, Blair, I would have expected a sounder commercial judgement.'

Blair found himself wavering.

'OK. I accept that it's official this end, but what about the other end. Who's the purchaser?'

Burton shrugged.

'The United Arab Emirates, I presume. We're doing it through a purchasing agent.'

Blair had a vague feeling there was something called an 'end certificate' to prove that the arms were going to stay in the country where they landed, but he couldn't be sure of his ground. He would have to check it later.

'We'd still have problems with the overflights, even if it's legit.'

'Then you'll just have to work out a route where no one complains,' Burton said, glanced at his watch and rose to leave. He had only eaten the first course. 'Would you excuse me now, I have another appointment.'

Blair wondered whether this man ever finished a meal. Maybe it was his way of keeping slim.

'Perhaps you'd cost it out for me, Tony, and work out a trouble-free route. Let me know at the office by lunchtime tomorrow.' And he was gone.

As before, Monica made no attempt to leave with him.

Paul wrote his letters, prepared himself a light snack from his father's fridge and had just decided on an early night when the phone rang. It was an international call from Salisbury, Rhodesia.

Blair gave Monica a lift back to her apartment block because her husband had taken the car and there seemed to be no taxis around. He had not intended to go on up to the penthouse that night, but somehow Monica seemed to expect it.

Over a nightcap of coffee and cognac she mentioned casually that her husband's appointment was in Edinburgh.

He had gone up on the late shuttle.

They talked business a while, small talk a while, and then, quite suddenly, Monica glanced at her watch and said, 'Are you staying the night or not?'

It seemed more attractive than the long drive home. A great deal more attractive.

They went to the bedroom without a word and undressed in the light. She changed her husband's pillow for a fresh one. It was a thoughtful gesture.

He made love to her but knew he had not been very good. When it was over she closed her eyes and addressed the ceiling.

'Do you want to leave now?'

'No,' he said.

'You're a liar.'

He made no move. A few moments later she was asleep.

She was still asleep when he woke at six. He had the airline pilot's built-in time clock. He rose and used the pulse shower. Noisily.

She watched him emerge through half closed lids.

A well-built ape, she thought, but already starting to run to fat. It didn't bother her. She didn't really like thin men. Not as good in bed as Charles. Too slow and ponderous. Charles was dedicated to giving her pleasure, just as he was dedicated to everything he tackled. This man was self-indulgent. But he might improve with practice. She wondered how much practice he had had. A girl in every airport, presumably. Black, white, yellow, brown. Fly me, I'm your handsome flight captain. She hoped he wasn't diseased. Though it might be fun to pass it on to Charles who, in all innocence, would pass it on to that red-haired bitch of a personal assistant he had taken with him to Athens and this evening to Edinburgh. Not that she had positive proof about the red-head. She was simply reading the signs. When a man starts indulging his wife's lovers it usually means he's got something on the side himself and wants to assuage his sense of guilt. The trouble with

Charles was that he was never that straightforward. There was usually a much more involved reason for his behaviour. She would just have to wait and see.

Blair towelled himself vigorously and saw that she was now awake.

'I take it he knows,' he said.

He had been reading her thoughts.

She shrugged an elegant shoulder, as best she could in a reclining position.

'Tell me about your son,' she said, changing the subject.

He had mentioned Paul the night before, but only in passing.

'I'm getting to like him,' Blair said.

She laughed. 'Didn't you expect to? Isn't that the most natural thing in the world that a man should like his son?'

'I'd put him out of my life. We met as strangers,' Blair said.

'You don't cut the bloodknot that easily,' she said. 'Are you going to bring him into the business?'

The thought had passed through Blair's mind.

'It could be useful, he's an accountant.'

'That might just get up Kim Hayward's nose, of course. She's been doing the accounts up till now.'

'But not too well, according to your husband's auditors,' Blair said.

Monica smiled. 'Take no notice of that. Charles always pulls that ploy when he's trying to get hold of something cheap. He was actually very impressed with her.'

Blair reached for his underpants.

'What's the rush to get away?' she asked. 'When a man turns forty he's usually better after a night's sleep.'

Blair left at nine. She gave him five out of ten and a bonus mark for making her coffee.

When he drove back to Stanwick he felt totally relaxed. A lot of men would have lost respect for a woman who so obviously wanted to sleep with them. Blair was the opposite. He found that intimacy only increased his respect for a woman. Above all, he admired honesty, equally in women as in men. He had not been in the least put out when Monica told him he wasn't terribly good in bed. On the contrary, it gave him something to aspire to in the relationship. He hated women who pretended satisfaction in order to flatter the male ego. He liked to think his ego was made of sterner stuff. Somewhere in the back of his mind the warning bell was jangling, but it was muted that morning. It wouldn't be difficult to fall in love with a woman like Monica Burton, and to admit the possibility is to concede that the process had already started. He felt the sharp edge of excitement. He was entering a new danger zone. The lady in question was, after all, married to the man who now controlled his destiny. He was not in the least fooled by Charles Burton's apparent complicity.

Paul Blair had recognized Ray Mason the moment the two pilots had entered the office from the Ximbali trip, but at that time he had more pressing things on his mind. As he worked on the audit that morning, Mason now reminded him. When he was small, Mason had been a fairly frequent visitor to the cottage. Blair and Mason were friends, so it was quite natural. He had played games with the boy and even helped him with technical advice when he was setting up his radio shack in the old summer house. He had always liked Mr Mason and looked forward to his visits. His mother had also liked him and occasionally he had called while his father was away. There had been nothing furtive in these visits. Paul, even at that age, had learnt to differentiate between his mother's callers. Alan McLeod would always park his car in the nearby village and walk the rest of the way. If he happened to bump into Paul on his way back from school he would always pretend a rather nervous 'fancy meeting you here' surprise. Mr Mason, on the other hand, drove right into the drive and thumped heavily on the door like the milkman calling for his money. Paul felt reasonably sure Mason was a genuine friend of the family. So the question that morning, Paul knew, was perfectly innocent.

'How's your mother keeping these days?'

'Fine,' said Paul in a neutral voice.

'Next time you write to her, give her my regards.'

'I will,' Paul said, and immediately changed the subject. They exchanged a few more reminiscences and Mason left him to get on with his work. There was no hint of resentment in his voice. No echoes of the quarrels between Mason and his father over the takeover. Either Mason was generous enough to feel that the sins of the fathers should not be visited on the children, or he had come to terms with the situation overnight. Paul hoped it was the latter. He liked Ray Mason and sincerely hoped that his father and Mason could stay friends. Certainly Mason seemed quite relaxed this morning. Even Kim Hayward, though not effusive, seemed helpful and bearing no grudge.

He completed the audit by lunchtime, joined his father at the bank and, half an hour later, Blair had his loan. By the evening, Tony Blair's half-share of Red-Air was safely in Mason's bank along with Burton's share. The company was at last legally theirs.

Paul did not ask his father why he had not come home the night before. He felt it was none of his business, and Blair did not volunteer anything other than it had got late so he decided to stay in town. Father and son dined out at the Eagle and Blair ordered champagne to celebrate the birth of the new company. He asked Paul if he would like to work for it and Paul was delighted to agree. Later they would work out his exact job. They arrived home late in fine spirits. Blair felt that his life was now full. He had half an airline, a fascinating mistress and a son who worshipped him and would help him succeed. He was a lucky man and a very happy man.

At just about the same time, Janet Blair landed at

Heathrow airport. The moment she had passed through customs she went to a phone booth, dialled her estranged husband's number and asked to speak to her son Paul.

4

As far as Charles Burton was concerned, Red-Air was now ready to roll. He felt quite pleased with the way things had gone so far. Taking over ailing companies tended to get easier with practice, and he had cut his teeth early in life. At fourteen, while still at the grammar school in the Wiltshire market town where he was born and reared, he had bought a Sunday newspaper round from a classmate. It had cost him a fiver – cut price because it was a particularly cold winter and paper rounds are a buyer's market in bad weather. By the time the spring came he had a daily round as well and four second-year kids working under him. The newsagent didn't really mind how the round was operated so long as their customers got their papers. In fact they considered him the best paperboy they had ever had. He was always the first there in the mornings and seemed to be able to handle his little band of red-nosed underlings far better than they could themselves.

He sold the round to a prefect for twenty pounds when the summer came and the market was high. With the proceeds he bought a larger round from a rival newsagent and took his obedient little workforce with him. The first newsagent was now left with no paperboys at all and by the time they had recruited more they found that little Charley Burton had poached nearly half their customers on behalf of his new employer. He had also increased his workforce, and by the end of the summer term had half the school second-year class working for him and two-thirds of the town locked up. He was taking fifty pence a week from each of the boys under his command and by the time he took his 'O'-levels was earning almost as much as his bank-clerk father. He left school at sixteen as he found it was wasting too much of his earning time. Within a year he had bought up the original newsagent's shop – it was now going broke for lack of child labour – using his father to sign the legal documents since he was still under age. He was now into the property business and on his eighteenth birthday sold the freehold of the shop to a chain store at a profit of £5000.

From then on there was no holding him. It was the time of the property boom and he bought and sold furiously, accumulating capital at each step until at twenty-one he found the town was too small to hold him and set out to try his luck in London. He also learnt the trick of diversifying. A small plastics factory on the Slough trading estate was bought and sold quickly again to finance a Bedford brickyard which generated enough capital for a paper mill near Leicester. Unfortunately it was a lulu and cost him £100,000 of his own money when it went to the wall. Only a fortuitous marriage to the daughter of a wealthy whisky distiller on Speyside saved his bacon by replenishing the coffers.

The marriage ended in divorce when he was thirty-two, and was without issue except for a sizeable package of shares in the distillery that had been part of the dowry. It was this interest that had taken him up to Edinburgh the night his second wife Monica was sharing his bed with Blair. The distillery, against the run of the normally healthy whisky market, was in trouble. In fact, several of the companies in his widespread portfolio seemed to be in trouble. U K industrials were going through yet another of their all too frequent bad patches. Time, he felt, to concentrate on his growing interests overseas. And time to generate some quick cash. Hence Red-Air with its promise of rapid cash flow.

After launching an overnight rescue operation with his ex-father-in-law, with whom he had remained on good terms, he caught the first shuttle back to London. His chauffeur took him straight to the penthouse. He arrived an hour after Blair had left. The smell of Blair's pipe tobacco still lingered in the air. But he made no mention of it. Kissed his wife fondly, showered and changed rapidly, glancing at the bed in passing to note that Monica had made a hasty attempt to make it, then left for his office. When he had gone, Monica examined his travelling suit for tell-tale red hairs. There were none, but then Charles was a careful man. Either that or the bitch wore a cheap wig.

Installed in his office behind his comforting bank of telephones, Burton called his friend, the rear-admiral, to arrange for the despatch of the first batch of the arms shipment to Stanwick airport by road, called his contacts in Abu Dhabi to advise them it was on its way, then put a call through to Athens to a third party involved in the deal. A party Blair knew nothing of. Neither, for that matter, did the rear-admiral.

The phone call from Janet that had shattered Tony Blair's idyll also shook his confidence in Paul. Had he known his mother was coming to England, if so, why had he not mentioned it? The boy swore he had not, though admitted taking a phone call from her twenty-four hours earlier.

'Why the hell didn't you tell me?' Blair asked angrily.

'I would have done, but you didn't come home that night,' Paul said.

'We've been together all afternoon and evening, you could have told me then!'

'I didn't want to spoil things,' Paul said, averting his eyes. 'We were so enjoying ourselves.'

'Then you *did* know she was coming.'

'She didn't say that. She just rang to ask how I was and what I was doing. There was no hint of anything else.' Paul had been making his own calculations. After she put the phone down, his mother must have headed for Salisbury airport within the hour or she could never have made it this quickly.

'How did she know where you were?' Blair persisted. 'You must have been in contact before.'

Paul conceded that he had written to her on arrival to say he was going to stay with his father. Then immediately wondered why he was apologizing for the fact. 'She *is* my mother, after all.'

Blair backed down straight away. He was being unfair. 'Of course. I'm sorry. There was no reason why she shouldn't know.'

At the same time he had a strong feeling that the boy was holding something back. A suspicion passed through his mind that the whole thing had been prearranged before Paul left Rhodesia. The son would go ahead to try and soften him up for something, then the mother would follow. Janet had always worked deviously when she wanted something. But what *could* she possibly want after all these years? No, he was doing his son an injustice by suspecting collusion. The boy was clearly upset by the news.

Another thought struck him. 'Do you think she's coming over to persuade you to go back with her?'

'I don't know,' said Paul. 'I don't know what she wants.'

But he had a strong suspicion. He just couldn't find the courage to tell his father.

The CAA inspectors arrived without warning, as was their practice. Kim knew them by sight, they were attached to Stanwick. She hurried into Mason's office to warn him.

'Ray, I've got a feeling we're being taken to the cleaners.'

'Who is it this time?' Mason got up from his desk and sighed.

'Captain Edwards with his engineering and air-frame men,' Kim said.

Mason followed her back into the traffic office to find them waiting for him, stone-faced. Edwards was a senior captain in his mid-fifties. A one-time regular fleet captain for British Airways Cargo Section, he was known as one of the toughest men in the CAA Inspectorate. He had an uncanny instinct for nosing out trouble. His two younger colleagues were equally skilled in their specialized fields. Together they formed a formidable team with the power to ground any aircraft at Stanwick if they found the slightest thing wrong with it.

Mason greeted Edwards cautiously.

'Hullo, Bob, what's on?'

'You weren't planning to take that Brit anywhere for the next forty-eight hours, were you, Ray?'

'Yeah, we're just checking Air Traffic Control for an Abu Dhabi run.'

'Sorry about that,' Edwards said without sounding very sincere about it. 'Afraid you'll have to postpone it.'

'You did us over a month back,' said Mason. 'What's this one in aid of?'

'Change of ownership,' said Edwards opaquely and left it at that.

Mason knew there was no point in protesting any further. On second thoughts, why the hell should he care? It wasn't his company anymore. As he walked out with the three men to the apron he smiled to himself as he thought of Burton's reaction. They had just been notified that the cargo for Abu Dhabi was due to arrive in two hours. Now it would have to wait in the sheds for the next two days.

Kim phoned Blair at home who broke the news to Burton. Burton practically blew a blood vessel over the phone and immediately cancelled all of his other appointments for the rest of the day. He called his chauffeur to take him down to Stanwick: this would have to be dealt with on the spot. He suspected foul play.

On arrival he marched straight into Mason's office and accused him to his face.

'Who called the bloodhounds in, you?'

'Why the hell should I?'

'To stop that plane taking off till you get your terms,' Burton snapped. 'It's a negotiating ploy, isn't it?'

Mason laughed. 'That's the trouble with devious buggers like you, Burton. You think everyone plays it as dirty as you do.'

'Then why should the CAA choose just this moment, when I've got a cargo all ready to go, to ground that plane for inspection?'

'Don't ask me, mate,' said Mason. 'Ask them.'

'I shall do just that,' Burton said tight-lipped. 'But I intend to go over their heads to the Inspectorate in London.'

Mason said he wouldn't get much change out of them, since they probably gave the instruction in the first place.

Burton said he was already familiar with some of the senior chaps up there, he had been in to see them when he first started bidding for Red-Air.

Mason burst out laughing.

'Then you've only got yourself to blame, mate. That's what set them on your heels.'

'Why should it?'

'Because you don't look like an air-freight man, Burton,' he said, enjoying the man's discomfort. 'You look like a well-heeled cowboy waltzing into the cargo business to make a quick killing, and they've decided to fire a warning shot across your bows. All right?'

Charles Burton was used to insults. He had learnt as a boy never to show anger. That only incited anger in your opponent and when you're three inches below average height you could end up minus a few teeth. Far more effective to couch your threats in the soft answer that turneth away wrath.

'Captain Mason,' he said amiably, 'I do hope you find you can come to terms with the new management, and co-operate with us in getting that plane in the air as quickly as possible. Otherwise we shall not be able to pay your salary.'

He turned and left, with the threat hanging in the air.

Outside on the tarmac he found Blair standing watching the inspectors as they started their inch by inch inspection of the Britannia. He asked if there was any possible chance of hurrying them up.

'No way,' Blair said. 'If you try and rush them they'll get suspicious and spend a week on it. There are half a million parts in that plane. Every one has to be checked against the log to make sure it's not time-expired or damaged. I wouldn't argue with those boys, my life depends on them.'

'And my contract depends on getting this arms shipment out to the customer without delay,' Burton said.

It was the first time he had actually used the word 'arms'.

'What's the rush?' Blair asked. 'Someone waiting to start a war?'

He was nearer the truth than he realized.

Despite the promptness with which Janet had phoned on arrival, she did not show up that day and made no further contact. Blair presumed she had some business in London. Paul seemed subdued and introspective. Blair guessed he was suffering from a conflict of loyalties and tried to take his mind off it by starting to integrate him into the complex procedures of the business.

It was agreed that the boy would take over the accounts. Blair sweetened the pill for Kim Hayward by appointing her company secretary and increasing her salary. Burton approved the appointment and raised no objection to the suggestion that Mason be designated operations director. This left Monica's job to be determined. As a journalist she seemed the right person to take over responsibility for publicity and public relations. She agreed, since she could do this part-time. Burton insisted that he should be in charge of sales for the time being, though everyone should regard themselves as salesmen in one way or another. It was their job to sell the image of Red-Air as a newly constituted, go-ahead freight company with a bright future. Burton gave them a little pep talk on that subject at a hastily convened first board meeting over lunch. No one else had much chance to comment since he was, as usual, dashing off to another appointment.

However, there was a lot to be done despite the aircraft being on the ground. A route had to be worked out for Abu Dhabi which gave them the minimum trouble with overflights. It was decided to fly due south, coast-hugging Spain outside the territorial limits, then through the straits and across the Mediterranean to Alexandria. This gave them maximum travel over neutral water with only Egypt and Saudi to clear. Egypt was dicey over clearance but since the Sadat/Begin honeymoon had ceased to bother too much that the cargo might be bound for Israel or the aircrew Jewish. The roundabout route would increase the cost due to a heavier fuel load and more aircrew flying time, but Burton didn't seem bothered about the extra expense. The only argument arose over the 'end certificate', the guarantee that the point at which the freight was to be unloaded was, in fact, the final destination. Mason wanted to see a copy of it, but Burton insisted that it was his business and nothing for anyone else to worry about.

The freight arrived by road and was duly stored in the sheds. Blair opened the crates to inspect the contents but could not make head nor tail of them. It was certainly highly sophisticated equipment, and appeared to be something to do with rocketry, presumably the computerized brains behind the weapons, but no weapons themselves and no explosives to make it a hazardous load. On the other hand, it was only a part load. He wondered what else was to come.

In the meantime the three CAA inspectors were busily removing panels and engine cowlings from the Britannia and generally treating it like a heart transfer patient on an operating table. At the end of the day Captain Edwards came over to Blair to tell him they wanted to give the plane an air test the following morning.

That night Blair dreamt of Janet. He was on the flight deck of a plane. He recognized the plane as a Britannia, yet the cabin area appeared much larger. All the controls seemed to be just beyond his reach. He strained against his harness but his fingertips would not quite touch. He glanced across the instrument panel and noted that all four engines were at full power, yet the needles on the fuel gauges were at zero. He looked at the artificial horizon and watched fascinated as it turned a full circle in front of his eyes. He felt cold and looked up to see if the heaters were on. It was then that he became aware of the face at the window. It was Janet's face, peering through the screen. He felt no sense of alarm, only curiosity. Dimly, in the back of his mind he knew she should not be there. The plane, he knew, was flying at 29,000 feet. She seemed to be speaking to him but he could not hear it. He told her to go away as she was obscuring his vision. A moment later her face disappeared and he was suddenly alarmed in case she had fallen off. She would be caught in the slipstream, he thought. He struggled with his harness until he was free, then found himself walking to the back of the flight deck. Again the same feeling of unusual space. He reached a bead curtain and pushed it aside. Now he was staring into cloud. The fuselage behind the flight deck had disappeared. Immediately it all made perfect sense. The artificial horizon had been rotating because the flight deck, severed from the body of the plane, was spinning. This seemed quite logical and he felt relieved that there had been no instrument failure. The air was warmer outside than it had been on the flight deck. A warm, balmy African night. He stepped out through the severed neck of the plane and his feet found soft earth. He was walking along a path that led through an endless kitchen. Pots and pans were neatly stacked and teacloths hung to dry on long lines. He was now in the basement of a huge hotel and could not find the exit. He turned back the way he had come and found swing doors.

He pushed them aside and was in a lift. Janet was in the lift with him. She put her arms round his neck and kissed him. She was naked and he could feel her belly pressed against him. He looked again and saw that it was Paul.

He woke in a cold sweat, turned on the bedside light and struggled out of bed. He was desperately thirsty. Crossing the landing to the bathroom he could see a spill of light in the hall below. He heard the sound of someone moving about and knew now that he was awake. He hurried downstairs to find the kitchen door partly open. Steeling himself against the possibility of a burglar, he pushed the door fully open and found Paul standing by the stove with his back to him.

Paul turned, startled, and gave a sheepish smile. 'I couldn't sleep,' he said. 'I'm sorry, Dad, did I wake you?'

Blair blinked in the strong light. He experienced a sudden moment of *déjà vu*. Then realized it was from his dream. The door, the kitchen. Janet – Paul. Paul – Janet. It must have been the sounds from the kitchen that had impinged on his dream in its last dying moments before he woke. He could not work out what the lift represented unless it was his passage to consciousness. His dream symbolism was usually fairly straightforward.

'Are you all right, Dad?' Paul was staring at him, anxiously.

'Yeah, fine. Are you making coffee?'

'Tea, would you like some?'

Blair nodded and glanced at his watch. It was four in the morning. It didn't seem worth going back to bed.

They talked together in the quiet intimacy of the small hours. Paul said he had hardly slept at all, anticipating his mother's arrival.

'Are you afraid of her?' his father asked.

Paul denied it, but admitted that she had a strong hold on him. She was possessive. He was the only child. He found it difficult to refuse her anything as she always dissolved into tears. Then he felt guilty.

'Then she hasn't changed much over the years,' Blair said. He was reminded of a phrase from *King Lear* – 'women's weapons, water drops'.

'Dad,' Paul said after a while, 'can I ask you a personal question?'

Blair smiled. 'I won't bite you.'

'Why didn't you marry again?'

'I suppose I couldn't think of a very good reason.'

'Well . . . company. Isn't that a reason?'

'I can get that on the flight deck.'

'I meant female company.'

'I can get that on the ground.'

'Didn't you ever feel like starting another family?' Paul said, watching his father's face closely.

'The world's overpopulated as it is, without me adding to it,' Blair said, then immediately realized his mistake.

'Does that mean I was an accident, then?'

'No,' said his father quickly. 'You were planned.' He hoped this was true so that the boy would not feel unwanted, but he couldn't quite remember. 'Did your mother tell you that you were an accident?'

'No,' said Paul. 'But she once admitted I was a surprise.'

'That was a bit harsh.'

'Not really,' Paul said with a lightheartedness that sounded hollow. 'I quite like the idea of being a surprise. It sounds a bit heavy being planned. Like being programmed. Parents expect you to behave according to the blueprint.'

Blair asked him if he was quite sure he wasn't following a blueprint by becoming an accountant. It sounded like Janet's idea.

Paul denied it. 'Mother didn't really mind what I took up so long as I didn't become an airline pilot.'

Blair laughed. 'So she saved you from a fate worse than death.'

'Actually, I would like to fly,' Paul said tentatively. 'I want to do a lot of things now I'm here. Race cars, water ski . . . all kinds of things I couldn't do out there. It was so stifling.'

So he really was a chip off the old block. Blair looked pleased, but surprised at Paul's old-fashioned idea of Britain as the land of golden opportunity for men of action.

'I thought it was all happening in Rhodesia these days,' he said.

Paul tried to explain that although he'd done his military service like all the other white Rhodesians of his age, he was just one of a crowd, acting under orders. He wanted to do something personal, something alone. 'Man against the elements.' It sounded gauche, but his father understood immediately. He had been the same at that age, ever since he had first read Saint-Exupéry, the French author and aviator who had regarded flying as a lone communication with the soul. Paul had read it too.

Christ, Blair thought. He's not just a chip off the old block, he's practically a bloody clone. And yet he'd turned out to be an accountant, of all things!

'But it's only in my imagination,' Paul added ruefully. 'I don't have your facility for turning dreams into reality.'

Blair was suddenly jolted into remembering his own dream. How she had kissed him in the lift and he had found her body warm and yielding. Why the hell hadn't he dreamt of Monica, or was he perhaps beginning to confuse the two in his subconscious mind?

'You can be whatever you want to be, Paul,' Blair said. 'There's only one trick to it. Act first and think about it later.'

'I don't think my mother would approve of that,' Paul said wistfully.

So he was still firmly under her thumb, despite his fantasies.

'Well,' said Blair to cheer him up, 'I don't suppose she'll be staying long. She'll want to get back to Alan.'

'I . . . don't think so,' said Paul. 'They've split up. I think she's here for good.'

He felt a wave of relief that he'd got it off his chest at last.

The Britannia nosed out on to the taxiway. Blair was glad to feel the old crate under his seat again. Edwards was standing behind the co-pilot. The engineering inspector was by the spanner's seat, the air-frame expert back in the hull where his sharp ears would be listening out for any unusual sounds of stress in flight. Blair found it hard to concentrate, his mind still full of the night thoughts of his ex-wife and the news that she was roaming free again. He responded to the tail-end of the routine taxi check automatically.

'Oil cooler flap controls . . .'

'As required,' Blair said.

'Pitot heat?'

'On,' said the engineer behind them.

'Flight recorder and transponder?' This was the captain's call.

'On,' said the co-pilot.

'On,' repeated the engineer.

'Flight fine pitch stops.' From the co-pilot.

'Checked,' said Blair and the engineer simultaneously.

'Landing lights?'

'Down and on,' replied Blair. That was the end of the normal taxi check.

Or should have been.

'Check readings on four,' Edwards said to his engineer.

Blair glanced sharply across at him from the pilot's seat. For some reason they must suspect the number four motor. No one had mentioned it to him. He could feel nothing wrong with it and the engineer's readback of the gauges confirmed that it was behaving normally. Edwards seemed satisfied and nodded to Blair to stand by. They got the clear from the tower, then both pilot and co-pilot put their hands on the throttles – a routine precaution – then they were away. Hunting 180 knots to clear the terminal buildings in a near perfect take-off. A few moments later, the white ribbon of the London to Stanwick motorway was a thousand feet below.

The driver of the rented Ford Escort nervously hugging the nearside lane did not look up as the plane passed overhead. She was too busy concentrating on her driving. It had been ten years since she had last driven in the UK.

According to the AA Handbook conveniently left in the glove pocket, the only hotel in the Stanwick area with a star rating was the Eagle. So Janet Blair checked in there. Before it had been modernized she knew it as the favourite haunt of air crews, so it was not mere coincidence that she chose it.

Dark, medium height, with the trim figure of a thirty-year-old, Janet was, in fact, past forty. Her face was tanned from the African sun. A handsome face, with full sensuous lips, a strong nose and deep-set grey eyes that seemed never to blink.

She wore a smart tailored two-piece, cream silk blouse and Italian court shoes. She was pleased with her new outfit and knew she looked good in it. Shopping for clothes in London again had been one of the delights she had missed for so long. Having her hair done in Bond Street was another. Idling over jewellery windows in the Burlington Arcade yet another. Had Tony Blair thought seriously about it he would have realized that the only thing that could possibly divert his ex-wife from whatever purpose she had in mind would be a London shopping spree. The delicious thought that all these goodies were now only an hour away instead of a continent away filled her with pleasurable anticipation. The English weather might be beastly and the service in the shops as atrocious as ever, but it was good to be back in the consumer paradise of Europe. Not that she was ever lavish in her spending, she felt. But she liked to buy things of quality when she did spend. It was so good for the morale.

She was pleased to find that the best room in the hotel, facing out on to the lawns, was free. She could not tell the receptionist how long she was staying. It would depend. She did not say what it would depend on, but simply left the sentence hanging in the air. Fate would decide that, though she might have to give it a nudge. She rang Blair's number from her room but there was no answer. She decided that Paul must be with his father somewhere and found the number of Red-Air in the telephone book. But it seemed to be constantly engaged, so she took off her shoes, lay back on the bed and did her yoga relaxation exercises. Within ten minutes she was asleep. She had the facility to drop off at any time of the day and wake completely refreshed. She would need her wits about her.

The first intimation Mason had that something was wrong came from Air Traffic Control. Red-Air Alpha Gulf, the Britannia's code sign, had called in from a position ten miles north of Flamborough Head to report an engine fault. They were now returning to Stanwick flying on three. It was then that the small Red-Air switchboard had been so busy that Janet had been unable to get through. Crash procedures had to be gone through, emergency services alerted. Nothing serious to worry about, Mason assured Paul. The Brit was perfectly capable of flying on three engines without loss of height or manoeuvrability, particularly when it was unladen. He had once landed her on two when both inner port and starboard motors had failed. His first reaction, in fact, was that it was a false alarm. Edwards might have deliberately cut the motor as part of the air test. But if so, they would not have reported it to the ATC. He heard the fire engines jangling away in the distance as they lined their noses up ready for the landing. They wouldn't be needed, he was sure, but it was good exercise for them.

Nothing at all to worry about, he assured an anxious Charles Burton on the line to his London office. But all the same, what the hell was going on? The motors might be old, but they had been well maintained. On the last trip all four had been running as sweet as a nut.

'Bloody typical,' he said to Kim. 'The CAA boys have to stick their thick thumbs in, prodding about all over the place, now they've buggered up one of my motors!'

He had an uneasy feeling it hadn't quite happened that way, but it reassured everyone in the office.

'*Your* motors?' Kim asked.

Of course. He kept forgetting. He was only an employee now. It was someone else's worry.

It was as Mason predicted. Although the Britannia had to stay in the air an extra hour to burn off fuel in case of a crash landing, it eventually came in spot down the centre of the glidepath to touch down with scarcely a bump. Blair had compensated for the oversteer with flaps and rudder, and an untrained observer would scarcely have known anything was wrong until the plane came close enough to see that one set of props was feathered. Even the normally truculent Captain Edwards felt obliged to give him a pat on the back as they nosed on to the taxiway.

'Couldn't have handled her better myself, Tony,' he said.

'I pass, do I?' Blair said. He had enjoyed the challenge.

'You do,' said Edwards. 'But not your plane, I'm afraid.'

The inquest went on all afternoon. By the time Burton and Monica arrived hotfoot from London, Blair, Mason and the three CAA inspectors were deep into an exchange of technical jargon that might just as well have been Albanian for all Burton understood of it. It appeared there had been something called a 'fifteen per cent oil pressure drop' and that the problems had started from there. Apart from discovering that there was an argument between Mason and the engineering inspector as to whether the fault lay in the motor itself or the instrumentation that recorded it, all Burton was able to determine was that the plane would have to stay grounded until the fault was traced, then given another air test to make sure it had been cured.

'How long is that going to take?' he demanded.

Blair shrugged. 'Depends what we find wrong. The fitters are stripping it down now.' He tried to reassure Burton, who was now starting to go grey around the gills. 'If it's just a minor fault, we can replace the part by tomorrow.'

'You'll be lucky,' said Edwards, reaching for his brief-case. 'If you want my opinion, that motor's US and only fit for scrap. I suspected it from the start.' He hurried away, his colleagues after him. They were already late for tea, and it wasn't their problem.

When they had gone, Burton drew Blair aside and demanded to know why no one had detected the fault before.

'Because it didn't arise before. A fault can develop any time.'

'Did you inspect the plane thoroughly before we bought it?'

'I'd just been flying it, hadn't I?' Blair said.

'That's not what I asked you,' Burton snapped. 'Did you give that plane a thorough engineering inspection before you came to me to raise the money to buy it?'

'Now wait a minute,' Blair interrupted. 'Let's get something straight. You wanted to buy in. I wasn't twisting your arm!'

'Just answer the question, Blair.'

Blair began to lose his temper.

'I'm not a bloody engineer. I'm a pilot. I checked the inspection logs, I talked to the spanners and I went by my own judgement from spending hundreds of hours in the seat! That's all I could do!' he shouted.

'In other words, at your recommendation, we bought a pup,' Burton said coldly.

'We bought a clapped-out old plane dirt cheap, Burton,' he said. 'And you knew it! It may need a few more spare parts, OK? That can happen any time and if you're going to wet yourself every time it does, you're going to be a pain in the arse. Now get the hell off back to London and leave me to sort it out!'

He strode off towards the sheds to supervise the fitters at their work. For all his dismissive reference to spare parts he had a nasty feeling that Edwards was right and they would need a new motor. There was a spare motor in the shed, but only the one. That too was old and there was no guarantee how much life it had in it. Much of the anger he had spent on Burton was due to the fear that he could be right. Perhaps they *had* bought a pup and Ray Mason had just got out from under in time. He stayed with the fitters for a while, but found he wasn't really much use. The job of dismantling a motor was a long and painstaking one. Nothing much would show up until the morning. He decided to go and eat. When he got back to the office to clean up he found Monica still there. Burton had gone back to town. She made an excuse that she wanted to stay on to prepare some sales publicity. In fact, he felt sure she had been waiting for him. Paul had gone home, she said.

They went to eat at the Eagle.

When Janet woke from her nap she bathed and changed, then tried Red-Air's number again. It was still engaged, but it didn't really matter. There was plenty of time. She had lunch, then took a drive around the countryside. It hadn't changed much in a decade except that there seemed to be fewer hedges and far more traffic on the roads. She drove through the village where she used to shop, stopped at the newsagent's for cigarettes, but no one seemed to recognize her. She drove on through the lanes until she reached the old cottage.

As she drew up, the first thing she saw was the estate agent's board announcing a sale by auction. She raised her eyebrows in surprise. Paul had not told her the auction date was so soon, only that his father had finally decided to sell the family home. She walked up the path and walked slowly round to the back. It seemed smaller than she remembered it. Perhaps it was because she had got used to the larger rooms of the big colonial farmhouse she had shared with Alan. It was certainly a great deal more neglected than in her time. The flaking paint on the windows, the broken guttering and the garden. How could Tony have let the garden run so wild? Not that he had ever cared much about appearances. A house was a place to sleep in after a long trip abroad. A garden was a place to sit in on the rare weekends he was off. And she had just been a wife to come back to after a few hectic nights in Beirut or Bangkok with whichever air hostess he could drag between the sheets.

She wondered if he was still at it. He'd be older now, of course, and presumably less attractive. Not that age ever seemed to worry those silly, footloose girls. Then she remembered with a wry smile she had been one herself once – a long, long time ago. She had done exactly the same, which is how she had first got landed with Tony.

She peered through the back window into the sitting room. He had got rid of the bergère and replaced it with a hideous modern vinyl suite. No taste. No taste at all. If it's functional, buy it. That had always been Tony's motto. The curtains too. Quite revolting. Had he no sense of colour clash?

She tried the back door and found to her surprise it was on the latch and unbolted. Careless as ever. She hesitated a moment, then walked in. Why not? A burglar could have wandered in, so why not an ex-wife who had laboured so long to make the place fit to live in? She had scraped down these walls and re-papered them. Still there, the same William Morris paper, but fading now. Her choice of furniture, or what was left of it. She had helped lay the woodblock floors and spent endless hours keeping them polished. Covered in some awful lime-green fitted carpet now. How *could* he? Too lazy to get down on his knees, she supposed.

What had happened to Mrs Thing? There was a vague evidence she still called – or *some* equally indolent Mrs Thing must pay an occasional visit. A hoover was left out in the hallway and Tony never used the hoover. But there were inches of dust on the bookshelves and the tops of cupboards. Smear stains three-quarters of the way up the kitchen walls where someone had reached with a wet rag but couldn't be bothered to get some steps and reach any further. A new fridge, badly iced up. The oven had not been cleaned inside for months. The cold-water tap was still dripping. God, she thought, it surely couldn't have been dripping for ten years! The crockery cupboards were practically empty. What could have happened to the Coalport dinner service they got from her parents as a wedding present? Two saucers left. He must have broken the rest over the years. Or smashed them all in one great angry outburst after she had left him. If he had cared that much, of course. She could never be quite sure. Or perhaps invited all his old pals in to celebrate and they had smashed the crockery piece by piece in some wild orgy.

Suddenly she found the atmosphere in the kitchen too overpowering. It reminded her of all those lonely anxious hours. She went back into the hall and slowly climbed the stairs. The bathroom was a disgrace. Doubtless it looked all right to him; Tony, who boasted near perfect vision, seemed incredibly short-sighted when it came to tidemarks around the bath or squashy bits of old soap in the shower tray, or rust stains on the radiator where he had dried his socks without ever wringing them out. How many times had she told him not to put wet things on the radiator? That was one thing she had never had to worry about with Alan. He didn't have that silly airline pilot's habit of washing out his own underwear as though home was just another hotel room. Not that it would ever have occurred to Alan. It was the job of the black servants. That was one thing she would miss now she was in England. Black servants. Just as well perhaps. It had begun to get difficult at the end and in any case, she reminded herself, she didn't really approve of the blacks being treated the way Alan always regarded them. It was one of the reasons why things had gone to pieces – her white liberal conscience.

She crossed the landing to the bedrooms. Paul, she noted, was installed back in his old room, but had hardly unpacked. No point if the house was to be sold. Well, that business had to be sorted out later. She hesitated before entering her old bedroom. No, *his* bedroom. But she went in just the same. Pickle. She might have guessed. He always dropped his clothes in heaps and expected her to hang them up. Same white melamine double wardrobes, but a handle missing and replaced with a piece of bent wire from a coathanger. Same four-poster bed they had picked up at the sale for forty pounds. But clean sheets. Amazing! A minor accolade to Mrs Thing. Or perhaps he's been expecting a brand-new air hostess. No, unlikely with Paul staying here – unless Tony had inducted him into his way of life already. She had a passing vision of father and son sharing the same mattress with a silly fat blonde from KLM with a big white Dutch bum.

It was then that she heard the key turn in the latch downstairs. How long had she been here, for God's sake? She looked at her watch, it was quarter to six. A whole afternoon had somehow disappeared in haunting a life she had long left behind. How perverse nostalgia could be.

She crept quietly out of the bedroom to the top of the stairs and looked down. It was Paul. He had not seen or heard her as he passed on through to the kitchen. Her instinct was to call out, or walk slowly down the stairs to greet him with a faintly reproving smile, but she decided against it. In Paul's eyes she would have no right here.

Without rights she would lose dignity. She would prefer to meet him on more neutral ground. She held her breath as he crossed below her from the kitchen to the sitting room. A moment later he switched on the television to hear the news. It gave her the sound cover she needed to slip quietly down the stairs and out through the back. He would have seen a car parked outside, but it could have belonged to the cottage opposite. She got in hastily and drove back to the Eagle.

Monica and Blair found a table for two in the far corner where they could talk undisturbed. They discussed mundane business matters for a while, the design of a new logo for the company, the preparation of a simple straightforward brochure explaining in layman's language just what services Red-Air had to offer and the advantage of a small outfit that could offer a more personalized service. But soon they were back on a more familiar basis. She told him she had been worried about the motor failure that morning – not so much for the plane's sake, but for his safety.

'Mason seemed to pass it off as a routine hazard,' she said. 'I had an uneasy feeling he was whistling in the dark. Was he?'

'So long as it was only one engine out, he knew we could handle her,' Blair said. 'The real problem is that, for all you know up there, whatever caused the first motor to go on the blink could affect the second or third. Ray would have known that, but it's his job to keep up morale on the ground.'

'So you could have crashed,' she said anxiously.

Blair laughed.

'Flying is a constant battle against the forces of gravity,' he said. 'And they never let up for one moment.'

'But it never bothers you.' She thought back to his cool, easy handling of the take-off from Ximbali. Was courage simply no more than a lack of sensitivity?

'Rubbish,' said Blair. 'Every one of your five senses is heightened in a crisis. Your eyes are watching the dials, your ears are tuned to the slightest variation in sound and your hands are busy with the switch mechanisms. Even your sense of smell is more alert. It's the only time you know you're really alive.'

Monica raised an elegant eyebrow.

'The *only* time?'

He thought about it for a moment.

'Yes, I think so.'

'You don't feel that when you're making love,' she said, then added, to make it sound casual, '. . . for example.'

'Not to the same degree,' Blair said.

'What a painfully honest man you are,' she said. It didn't really sound like a compliment.

'Simple scientific facts,' he said. 'A plane has to be handled more delicately than a woman. She's not full of kerosene.'

'Now I know why your marriage broke up,' Monica said tartly. She was starting to be sorry she'd shown concern for this man. He was clearly too self-possessed to need it.

'Mind you,' Blair added insult to injury, 'some have a higher flashpoint than kerosene. But I've never met a woman yet who could melt metal.'

Haven't you, you arrogant bastard, she thought. We shall see. She abruptly changed the subject.

'You seem to have upset Charles,' she said. 'What was all that about?'

'I just told him to get off my back. I had enough to worry about.'

'So has he,' Monica said. 'After all, he's gone to a lot of trouble and expense lining up business for the company. There was no need to be quite so rude.'

It was the first time since they'd met that Blair had known her take her husband's side. He must have upset her.

'Come off it, he's lining up business for himself. Red-Air happened to fit conveniently into the picture. In fact, I think he had the arms deal lined up first and only came into my deal as an afterthought. Right?'

She admitted this was partly right. Blair felt this was the time to try to get something sorted out between them that had been worrying him.

'So all that bit about trying to get me launched because he was grateful for me saving your life at Ximbali was just bullshit.'

'Not entirely,' Monica said. 'He's more complicated than that. He can really only express gratitude in commercial terms, but instinctively made sure you could both benefit.'

Blair said it reminded him of his father who bought him a train set as a child but was actually buying it for himself and insisted he was the only one who knew how to work the signals.

'All right,' Blair said. 'That's Charles sorted out, now what's *your* role in all this?' He felt he now knew Monica well enough to demand the truth.

'I fancied you,' she said, making no bones about it. 'Still do.'

'Not just because I could be useful in your old man's commercial enterprises,' he asked.

She coloured. 'I don't pimp for Charles, if that's what you think,' she said angrily. 'As a matter of fact I'm not even sure you *are* useful! You're as unsubtle as a barn door, both in business and in bed.'

Blair felt as though he'd been poleaxed. Honesty was one thing, but this lady knew how to hurt.

'Not a lot of point in fancying me then, is there?' was all he could muster in defence.

How easy it was, she thought, not for the first time in her life, to cut a man down to size by impugning his virility. But she didn't really want that with Touy Blair. He was too vulnerable. It was taking sweets from a child. She knew she would have to let him restore his dignity a little or she'd lose him altogether.

'You're an ape,' she said. 'But a handsome ape. Perhaps every woman needs an ape in her life.'

That made him feel better. She could see it in his face. She half expected him to leap up from the restaurant table and start thumping his chest. Instead he suddenly seemed distracted. His eyes had been caught by someone who had just entered the restaurant. Monica followed his gaze. A woman. She might have known. The bastard was falling back on lesson one in the male chauvinist textbook. Once a woman admits a weakness for you, start showing interest in another. How simple-minded could you get!

The brunette returned his look and smiled.

Cheeky bitch.

'Old flame?' Monica asked sweetly.

'Ex-wife,' said Blair, not moving a muscle to return Janet's smile.

'That should brighten up the evening,' Monica said with genuine pleasure. 'Ask her to join us.'

5

One day, Blair thought, someone will invent a new board game that will make Monopoly look like noughts and crosses. It will comprise two intelligent women, highly versed in the art of concealing their true feelings, and one rather bewildered man. It will probably be called something like Triangle, for only three can play. It would have one disadvantage as a game of chance, predictability – for the man is bound to lose. On second thoughts, perhaps it should be called The Castration Game.

He did his best to stay in play but he was on a hiding to nothing. Monica had made the opening move by inviting Janet over to join them with a friendly greeting. The two women then delicately manoeuvred themselves into their positions by somewhat over polite interest in each other's decorations.

'What a fascinating pendant,' Monica said, examining some strangely carved object hanging from Janet's neck by a gold chain. 'Is it African?'

'Namibian, actually,' said Janet. 'I'm so glad you like it. Most people think it's a bit gruesome.'

Both scored on the round. Monica for appreciating, Janet for appreciating her appreciation. Each collect 200 points for passing 'Go'.

Blair thought he'd get off with a funny.

'It's a shrunken head,' he said.

Both women greeted the remark with contemptuous silence.

Go to jail, fool, and miss two turns.

Janet's move now. An apparently innocent remark

about finding a good hairdresser embraced a compliment to Monica's own hairstyle.

Then the menu card was brought into play.

'Would you like to order?' said Monica. 'I can recommend the bouillabaisse.'

'Sounds delicious,' said Janet. 'Just what I feel like.' She thanked Monica for the suggestion.

'Tony, can you signal the waiter?' Monica said, thus establishing that he was her man at the table and did her bidding.

Ah, out of jail already, thought Blair. If only to perform a function. He called the waiter and ordered the bouillabaisse. Immediately Janet changed her mind and asked for dover sole, so rejecting Monica's choice that a moment ago was just what she felt like.

Honours even. Both women throw sixes.

'Then I'd better order a bottle of white,' Blair said. There was claret on the table.

'No, I'm still on Perrier, darling,' Janet said, as though he could be expected to remember that from a decade ago.

Go back to jail, Tony, and watch the play. He noted her counter-move by calling him 'darling', so establishing this was her prerogative.

'Tony tells me you've been living in Rhodesia,' said Monica. 'How exciting.' Translated, this meant 'I am Tony's confidante, he's told me all about you.' Now the game was hotting up.

Janet chose to take it as an intellectual challenge and the two women discussed the political changes taking place in Southern Africa, the decline of white rule, the emergent consciousness of the black Africans and how Janet had coped with her own change of lifestyle. They were now cautiously sounding each other out on the colour question. Monica seemed delighted that Janet seemed to share her own liberal standpoint. Blair thought of asking his ex-wife why she had quit the country when white rule ended since she approved of a multi-racial society, but he was now so far behind the play that he thought he'd best keep out of it. Janet congratulated Monica on being so terribly well informed for an outsider and Monica explained that she was a journalist.

Now it was Janet's turn to be fascinated. Or appear to be.

Blair decided to get drunk. They were now being so sweet to each other it was positively sickening.

He ordered another bottle of claret while they discussed the ethics of journalism, newspaper attitudes towards Africa, et alia, et alia.

Both women seemed to know instinctively when that round had come to an end. They had now been round the board once and it was time for one of them to draw a chance card.

Monica just reached it first.

'Will you go back?' she asked casually.

Janet appeared to ponder the question for a moment.

'There doesn't seem to be really anything to go back for,' she said earnestly. 'Now that Paul's here. After all,' she shrugged vaguely, 'he's my family.'

'So what are you going to live on?' said Blair. It was a crude intervention and both women glanced at him witheringly as though he'd just upset the board.

'Oh, I'm all right,' Janet smiled, then called to the waiter for coffee.

Monica said she would have to go. She had a long drive back up to town. But before Blair could even fold up his napkin, added quickly, 'In any case, you two must have an awful lot to talk about after all these years.'

She then told Janet how nice it was to meet her and she hoped they would see each other again. Janet said she hoped so too. Then Monica turned to Blair and said, 'I'll see you in the office tomorrow, Tony.' And she left. She had scored the final point, but both women knew that the game had really only just started.

When Monica had gone, Janet said, 'Congratulations.'

'For what?'

'For finding yourself such a very attractive and intelligent lady,' Janet said.

'All right, Janet, what do you want?' he said bluntly.

'Coffee,' she said. 'This is a very slow waiter.'

'That's because he's white,' said Blair. But sarcasm was always lost on Janet.

He again asked her what she had come back to England for and again she avoided answering him.

'Let's talk about you,' she said. 'Tell me what you've been up to.'

He got up from the table.

'I've had a tiring day,' he said. 'I'm going home to bed.'

He paid the bill for all three of them, refusing her request to put it on her bill, said a brief 'Good night' and walked out.

Janet seemed completely unperturbed by his sudden departure. She was quite used to it.

Outside the Eagle, Blair hurried to the car park, but Monica had already left.

He slept uneasily that night.

Ray Mason had more on his mind than the problems at Red-Air. By nature and disposition he was a strong family man. He had married Audrey when they were both in their early twenties and both had immediately fulfilled the marriage vows by forsaking all others. It wasn't that either of them were particularly religious or dutiful, but Audrey was soon into child rearing and Ray reckoned he already had more than enough on his plate without going through the hassle of marital infidelities. They had two boys, John and Gerry, now thirteen and fourteen respectively. John was a plodder, like his father. Nothing came easy to him, but he worked hard at school and spent long industrious hours over his homework.

Gerry was quite different and Mason felt it hard to believe he was theirs; sometimes he wondered if there'd been a cot switch at the maternity home. Small of stature and sharp of mind he had the manic energy of a hobgoblin. One day when he was a baby, he was on his back, the next he was up the cot side like a monkey and running across the bedroom. When he fell flat on his face, his mother ran to pick him up and asked her little mannikin soothingly what on earth had made him do that. He looked at her accusingly, stubbed a chubby finger in her belly and said 'You!' It was the first intimation that he could talk. He was clearly a bright and intensely logical child, for as his mother reasoned proudly afterwards, the boy's rapidly expanding intelligence had immediately grasped the fact that since it was his mother who had given him birth, it must be her fault that he had fallen on his little elfin face. It was a philosophy he was to develop to a fine art as he came to grips with the world.

Mason had been doing well when the boys were in their early childhood. He had two planes operating and a full order book. They bought a fine old early Victorian house on the edge of Stanwick village with a carriage sweep, half an acre of lawn and walled vegetable garden. Audrey insisted that the boys should go to private schools after their nursery years. Mason would have been quite happy with the local village school, but was overruled. John did well in his own steady way, but Gerry started making rapid strides within weeks and seemed to shine in every subject he tackled. Audrey was convinced the boy was a budding genius, but her husband wasn't quite so sure as the lad never seemed to do any work. Just occasionally, when he had been consistently getting high marks in a subject, he would suddenly come bottom in the next test. Audrey put it down to the onset of puberty and the odd periods of inattentiveness one might associate with genius. If his teachers knew any other reason, they weren't letting on.

Then came the change of fortunes. As Mason's business went steadily into debt he was no longer able to afford private education for his sons. It would have to be the nearby comprehensive. Ray Mason quietened his wife's fears that they would instantly turn into little vandals, and secretly he was pleased. He couldn't stand the snobbery of the other parents and their children at the private school.

John rode the change easily, but Gerry was beaten up by the other kids until he learnt to drop his posh accent. His end-of-year report, however, was even more curious than before. His school essays were now in the local vernacular and his exam marks even more widely ranging. The crunch came when a school project he had been working on all term was marked C minus. His mother considered the marking so grossly unfair she dragged her husband along to the school to tackle his form master. The man was obviously an idiot and hadn't bothered to read it.

But he had. Twice. Once in its original form under brother John's name, the second time under Gerry's name with a few sentences added and a smarter cover. She instantly assumed John had been cribbing from his brilliant brother. The form master shook his head. 'Your son Gerald,' he said wearily, 'is the most accomplished cheat it has ever been my misfortune to teach. He hasn't got a single original idea in his head.' Then added, to cheer her up, 'But he does have one rare talent. He genuinely believes it is all his own work. The boy should go far.' He hoped it would be somewhere like the Falkland Islands.

When Audrey got over the shock she started to rationalize. Since the private school had never accused her star-bright child of cheating, it was perfectly obvious he must have picked up the habit from the other little villains in the state school. Ray's fault for sending the boys there. She would take both boys away forthwith and find them a decent public school where the public couldn't corrupt them. Ray would jolly well have to find the money from somewhere.

This was just at the time that her husband was forced to sell out to Burton and Blair, so when Burton told him he either had to co-operate in the new set-up or draw no salary, this new burden was heavily on his mind. He would now have over £5000 per annum to find after tax. He had no choice but to play ball. It would have eased the burden a bit if he could have shared his troubles with Kim Hayward, but she was no longer a sympathetic ear. Ever since she had been appointed a director she seemed to have fallen increasingly under Burton's spell. When it came to a vote over an issue in dispute she would glance apprehensively towards Burton as though silently seeking his guidance on which way to cast her lot. Mason remembered the conversation they had had in the bar at the Eagle when she had told him to be clever and play it her way. Perhaps she was just being subtle, but Mason was getting increasingly uneasy about her. There seemed to be some invisible bond between her and Burton that he couldn't fathom.

Tony Blair carefully avoided going near the Eagle all that week so as not to bump into Janet. He knew she must be in contact with Paul, but the boy never mentioned it and his father didn't ask. In any case he was far too busy to worry about emotional problems. Edwards had been proved right. When they got the faulty motor on the test bed it proved to be too far gone for repair and they had to fit the spare. This involved further delays before the plane was finally passed fit to fly. Even then Edwards warned that in his view it was on its last legs. He gave it about a hundred more flying hours to live, if that. But it was anybody's guess.

Blair had plenty of other things to think about. He had to recruit additional crews and spent many weary hours talking to pilots, first officers and engineers. Most of them were either past their prime or inadequately experienced on turbo-props. The best of them would take a long look over the aged Britannia and make excuses that they had other interviews to go to and would let Blair know. Few ever did. He ended up with a forty-five-year-old Aussie who had been flying for Air Nugini and Blair suspected had a bottle problem. But his qualifications were good and Blair liked him for freely admitting he'd been fired for landing a Fokker Friendship at Port Moresby with more whisky in his belly than fuel in the tanks. He swore he had now been dried out for a year and Blair decided to take a chance. The remainder of the two crews was made up either from young ex-RAF men or crewmen that Blair had known from his own flying experience.

The Brit was now ready to make its first flight to Abu Dhabi, to Burton's obvious relief. Blair would like to have flown the trip himself but was too tied up, so he gave it to the Aussie pilot, Lee Robertson, with Don Saunders as his first offlcer. It took off without a hitch. At three in the morning, Blair was woken up at home by a telephone call.

'Tony, it's Lee.' Blair shook the sleep from his eyes. It sounded like trouble.

'Where are you?'

'Where you bloody sent me, mate. Up the arse end of the Persian Gulf.'

'Everything all right?' Blair asked anxiously down the phone.

'Yeah, no sweat, but I'm having a bit of up and downer with this Greek.'

'What Greek?' Blair said.

'Dunno. Calls himself Nick, but they're all called bloody Nick. He's offering me five grand to fly the freight on over the Gulf. Are we interested?

'Where to?' Blair said.

'Some military airstrip. He's being a bit cagey about it, reckons it's a five-hundred-mile round trip,' Robertson said.

'Tell him to get lost,' Blair said. 'Dump it, get your papers signed and head back.'

'You're the boss,' said Robertson. 'Tell you what, though. Just bumped into an Ayrab in the whorehouse who wants to ship a load of carpets to Rome. They're customs cleared. Do you want it?'

'That I'll buy,' said Blair. 'But get the cash up front.'

'Right, mate. Give us a traffic clear for Rome and call me back.'

Then he hung up.

Blair was pleased with the Australian captain. He was showing just the kind of enterprise the company needed. He'd seen the chance of a payload on the return leg of the journey and grabbed it. Blair had offered his pilots a bonus if they used their own initiative in finding a back-leg load so long as they checked back with him first. But he was particularly pleased with the Aussie for reporting the attempted bribe.

He got dressed quickly and hurried down to the Red-Air traffic office to arrange the flight clearances for the unexpected Rome flight. As he drove through the night to the airport he tried to puzzle out what was going on out there in the Middle East. He knew nothing about any Greek, but supposed this was the handling agent Burton had talked about. A five-hundred-mile round trip across the Gulf would take the plane into Iran. Did Burton know anything about this? Blair spent the next couple of hours arranging the necessary clearances, overflights and landing permission for Rome, telexed the routing back to Robertson in Abu Dhabi, then telephoned Charles Burton. It was still only half past five in the morning, but Burton answered at the second ring, quite bright and clear.

'You didn't tell me that stuff was bound for Iran,' Blair said bluntly.

There was a fraction' silence over the phone, then Burton said, 'Iran? That's the first I've heard of it.'

Blair called him a liar and told him about the Greek and the bribe.

Burton listened quite unruffled, then said calmly that he imagined the Greek agent had some sort of deal on the side, but it was really much too early in the morning to discuss it, and hung up.

Burton made no further contact with the office and Blair had to wait until Robertson landed the Britannia back at Stanwick late that afternoon before he was able to get any more details.

It appeared that the Greek had met the plane the moment it arrived in Abu Dhabi, taken Robertson aside and complained bitterly that the payload was a week late, which had upset all the local arrangements. The Greek had been vague as to what those arrangements were originally, but the Aussie captain got the impression that some other carrier had been waiting to take the arms crates on to another destination, but whether by plane or by sea through the Gulf he had no idea. Neither did he know whether Iran was the final destination. They could have been routed on to Pakistan or even Russia or China for all he knew.

'Did he actually name the airstrip he wanted you to fly to?' Blair asked.

'No, he gave me some bullshit about it being a military secret and he'd come on the trip with me and tell me in the air. He swore he had a mate in traffic control who'd clear me through, but there was no way I was going to get caught on that one,' Robertson said.

Blair paid him his percentage for the Rome freight and thanked him for playing it straight and resisting the bribe.

'Wasn't big enough,' said the Aussie with a grin. 'If the mean bugger had offered me ten grand I might have had a go.'

As he left the office he said to Blair, 'What sort of a crook outfit is this, anyway?'

'It's a straight cargo operation,' said Blair.

'You could have fooled me,' said the Aussie. He looked rather disappointed.

The second batch of crates had arrived in the sheds from the naval depot that day. Blair went out to inspect them.

This time there was no doubt at all, they comprised the dissembled parts of a rocket launcher. Blair was determined they would not leave the country until he had forced Burton to give him all the facts – and in front of witnesses. He would call a board meeting.

Paul saw his mother on the second evening after her arrival. She invited him over to the Eagle but they had dinner at a local Chinese restaurant to avoid the possibility of Blair arriving. She wanted to be alone with her son. She tried her best to put him at his ease by keeping to neutral topics, news and gossip about people they knew in Zimbabwe-Rhodesia. She made no attempt to reproach him for leaving, on the contrary, as the evening wore on she said she thought it really for the best. He would have far more opportunities in the UK. She even said she was glad that he was working with his father.

He looked at her suspiciously. 'Is that really true, Mother?'

'Yes, Paul. And with Ray Mason. It means you're not amongst strangers. That's nice for you.'

'Ray sends his regards,' Paul said.

'Please thank him, and tell him I'll be seeing him soon. He's such a *nice* man.' 'Nice' meant a lot more things from Janet's lips than one could ever find in the *Oxford English Dictionary*. In her vocabulary it ranged from harmless and malleable to socially undesirable, but in this case she probably meant friendly to *her*.

'What a strange twist of fate that Ray should now be working for your father,' she went on. 'We were all such good friends years ago.'

Paul knew that fate would come into the conversation sooner or later.

'And now *you* working for them both.' She smiled. 'And *me* only a few miles away. It's odd how destiny completes a circle.'

Not in the least odd when you contrive it, he thought.

But it would have sounded rude and he knew better than to upset her.

'Have you seen the cottage since you arrived?' he asked, to change the subject.

'I drove past it,' she said, not mentioning that she'd been inside. 'It's looking a bit careworn, but still attractive. What a pity it has to be sold at last.'

'Dad needed the money,' he said. But if she heard the remark she didn't register it.

'I always think it's a shame when the family home has to go,' she went on.

Paul looked blankly at her. She really was amazing in her total disregard for reality at times.

'Mother, the family home broke up years ago,' he said.

'But you and your father are in it together again,' she said. 'That's a sort of partial reinstatement.'

Paul said it wouldn't be for long, they were moving to a flat.

'Whereabouts?' She sounded just a little too eager.

Paul said they were looking around, but his father really hadn't had much time to flat-hunt. In fact they had their eyes on a couple of places, but Paul felt he had better be vague about their exact location in case his father objected to her knowing.

They ended the evening on pleasantries.

The following day she rang him at work, sounding very excited and asked if he could spare an hour off. He came over in his lunchtime. She told him she had a surprise for him and whipped him straight off to show him a flat. She had got the keys that morning from the estate agents. She said she was sure it would be suitable for the two men, as it didn't need much looking after. When they got there, Paul found it was one of the flats he and his father already had the details of, but hadn't yet got round to inspecting. Paul told his mother this, but she appeared not to hear it. A few days later, Blair did, in fact, rent it since it was quite close to the airport, but for ever after Janet would be convinced she had found them somewhere to live when they were practically homeless.

The third time he saw her was the day he and his father moved in. They were just carting the last pile of books through the doorway when she strolled past.

'Oh, hullo,' she said breezily. 'New flat? What fun. Can I look round?'

'Help yourself,' Blair said. Paul hadn't told him she'd been round already. He knew she liked to play her own charades her own way. She inspected every room minutely, objected to the curtains as cheap and nasty, the carpeting in the main room as poor-quality nylon and the bedroom wallpaper too loud.

Apart from that, she said, it seemed very suitable, but they would need to get someone in to do the cleaning.

'Thanks for the advice, Janet,' said Blair drily. 'Now you can shove off.'

She collected her handbag and waited till she was at the door before delivering her punch line.

'Paul and I thought you'd like it, Tony,' she said, and disappeared down the street.

Paul, embarrassed, started to explain to his dad, but Blair cut him short. 'No need to apologize, son. I know your mother at least as well as you do,' he said. He also knew it was time he stopped avoiding her and took the bull by the horns.

The arms shipment wasn't the only payload on Red-Air's order books, though Burton seemed to behave as though it was. There were regular routine trips that Blair had taken over from Mason's own operation. What pilots called 'the veal run' for example. Stanwick was in farming country and every so often truckloads of calves would arrive to be corralled just beyond the sheds prior to being loaded on the Brit in pens and shipped off to Naples, Milan or Rome where veal fetched a higher price than in the UK. Sometimes it was full-grown cattle to replenish the herds in the new African states. This entailed very careful planning. Livestock had to be watered regularly and if the journey involved a fuel stop, unloaded and corralled at the stop-over point. Occasionally it would be prize bulls being sent overseas for stud purposes. They had to be treated with special care. An insecurely roped full-grown Ayrshire bull could be pretty frightening if it broke loose at 25,000 feet. A stray horn through the fuselage wall and the pressure would drop like a capsized balloon. No one had yet invented an oxygen mask you could hastily fit on a wild bull in flight, even if you could get near it. By the time the pilot got down low enough to restore the pressure balance he'd have a payload of cold beef to unload. Sheep were easier, both to load and carry, but hellishly noisy. But Mason always reckoned that pigs were the worst over long distances. Unable to sweat through their skins, all their moisture came out on their breath and before long the hold would be steaming like a pressure cooker, evaporated moisture running down the walls in rivulets. They also had to keep eating, and, by the same token getting rid of it just as fast. The stench in the hold after a pork run took days to get rid of, however much you hosed down and disinfected.

There was also occasionally live traffic on the return leg. As Africa had been Red-Air's regular tramp run, the Britannia had often returned with wild animals for European zoos or circuses. The hold ceiling height was too low for giraffes, but zebras, wildebeeste and Thompson's gazelle were not uncommon. These would be crated, but needed close and continuous attention. In this case there would be a trained handler with veterinary experience travelling with the flight. Reptiles were no great problem, unless one of them wriggled out of its crate and decided to come up for'ard and take a look at the flight deck. Mason once had a six-foot python paying him a visit over the Azores. He had just hit some cold-air turbulence and dropped suddenly 200 feet. One of the wooden crates he had taken aboard at Jo'burg must have literally jumped up in the air as the plane fell beneath it, broken its fastenings and split open. At the same time the interconnecting door to the flight deck had swung open. The first Mason knew of all this was when he put his right hand down to throttle back and touched something cold and clammy. A moment later the great snake's head was on his lap, baleful eyes staring up at him. He sat in his seat hardly daring to breathe for a full ten minutes while his first officer took over the controls on dual. Finally the flight engineer had the presence of mind to drop his jacket over its head and chop it through the middle with a fire axe. Flying cargo was not always as dull as it might sound.

When the Britannia got back this time from Abu Dhabi there were three racehorses waiting to be taken to France for the Longchamps races. Horses generally travelled well and were accompanied by a groom to keep an eye on them, so Blair let one of his young ex-RAF pilots cut his teeth on the trip. Safely loaded and away he drove up to town to Burton's office. Burton had insisted that he was too busy to come down to Stanwick and if Blair wanted a board meeting it would have to be at his place. Mason came up in his own car with Kim. Although the Red-Air offices had officially closed up for the evening, Paul stayed on to man the phone. There always had to be someone there while a flight was in progress, just in case of trouble. Monica was already in Burton's office when the rest arrived. Kim, as the new company secretary, made a brief report on finances. Expenditure still far exceeded income, but that was to be expected for the first few weeks. The future looked better, the order book seemed to be filling up. Blair in his report confirmed that they now had half a dozen flights laid on for the next fortnight, mainly short haul, but some indication that shipping and forwarding agents had restored confidence in Red-Air.

'You haven't included my shipments in that forecast,' Burton said from the chair.

'I'm coming to that in a moment,' he said. He reported the engagement of new office staff, ground loaders and air crews. He then went on to raise the question of spare parts.

'We were pretty thin on spares when we took over,' he said. 'But most of the things we need can be built up as and when we have cash available. But the one thing we must have is a spare motor. Two, if we want to be on the safe side, but it's just asking for trouble to operate without one at all.'

'What do they cost new?' Burton asked.

'The Proteus 255 has been phased out,' Blair said. 'The motor to replace it now costs a million and a quarter.'

'That's ridiculous,' Monica exclaimed. 'That's six times as much as we paid for the whole business, including the plane itself!'

'Ah, she's just cottoned on!' Mason said with heavy sarcasm.

Burton ignored him. 'What about these Aviation Exchange people, can't they find us one second-hand?'

'They're looking out for us,' Blair said. 'But it's not easy to find one in good working order. We may have to cannibalize.'

'What does that mean?' Monica asked.

'Look around the world for a Brit that's failed its test and is going for scrap and make an offer for the motors.'

'But if it's failed its test . . .' Monica began.

'It could have failed for half a dozen reasons, air-frame, hydraulics, anything. But at least one motor might be in good nick.'

'But how do you set about looking?' Burton asked.

Mason said, 'You just put it out on the grapevine. Aircrew travel all over the world, they hear things.'

'Or you watch out for reports of accidents,' Blair added.

Monica looked at him sharply.

'You sound like a jackal.'

Blair shrugged.

'Accidents happen. There's a plane piling up somewhere in the world every day of the week. It may not be fatal. If it was a serious crash it would be no use to us anyway. The motors would have burnt out. But if it's just damage to the air-frame on the ground you could be lucky.'

He now moved on to the real reason he had called the meeting.

'I appreciate that the chairman has provided us with a few lucrative payloads, and we need the money,' Blair said. 'But if we're getting into the arms traffic business, I want to be informed of every detail, including where it ends up.' He looked hard at Burton. 'Can we have that agreed and minuted, Mr Chairman?'

'We are a carrier,' Burton said. 'If you take the veal run to Milan, do you insist on knowing who eats it?'

'Arms are different,' Blair insisted. 'It's unfair to my aircrews to expect them to take those risks.'

'Then give them a bonus,' Burton said casually, 'or take those flights yourself, Tony. I know *you're* not afraid to take risks.'

Blair began to get annoyed.

'I'm managing director of this company, and I find it insulting to be kept in the dark. Why in hell aren't you prepared to tell me?'

'Because I haven't the slightest idea,' Burton said evenly. 'I really couldn't care less so long as the money's on the nail.'

'I think that's quite immoral, Charles,' Monica said. 'You're trading in human lives!'

'And supposing the arms are going to some liberation movement you happen to approve of, darling,' he said. 'Would you still think it's immoral?'

'But you just don't know,' Monica insisted. 'That's surely Tony's point.'

'Not quite,' Blair said. 'I'm thinking of the company's reputation and the safety of the crew. That's all.'

'Then you're no better than *he* is,' Monica snapped

back at him. 'And while we're on the subject of payloads, I don't think we should be carrying calves to slaughter in some filthy Italian abattoir!'

'If we don't do it, someone else will,' Blair said. He was starting to be sorry he'd raised the item.

She turned on him angrily. 'That's the kind of excuse Gestapo Kommandants made at the Nuremberg Trials. I would have expected some kind of a moral stand from you,' she said witheringly.

Blair couldn't think why, but there was no stopping her now.

She turned to Kim for support since she was only meeting glum faces from the men. 'Don't you agree?'

Kim said she always had felt sorry for the poor little calves, they had such sad eyes, but she supposed they had to die somehow.

Mason was enjoying this and decided to stir it up a bit more.

'They're going to a good Catholic country,' he said. 'All the veal cutlets go to the cardinals.'

'That's just the sort of stupid, facetious remark I'd expect from you,' Monica said, defending her female colleague as a matter of course. This was now turning into a battle between the sexes, Blair thought. Burton, he noticed, had suddenly gone quiet.

He tried being reasonable.

'All right, Monica, what kind of payloads do you think we should be carrying?'

'Food to the millions starving in the third world,' she said. 'Medicines and clothing to disaster areas.'

She flourished a copy of the *Evening Standard*. It carried a story about famine in South-East Asia. Oxfam and Save the Children Fund had issued an appeal for help.

'Why aren't we carrying relief supplies to these areas?' she demanded.

'Because no one's asked us,' Blair said.

'What's to stop you volunteering, for God's sake?'

There was a moment's shuffling, uneasy silence. Blair looked to the chairman for words of wisdom.

'I think Monica has made my point exactly,' he said amiably. 'The moment you start to get concerned about the purpose to which the goods we carry may be put, we end up in all kinds of contentious moral judgements. You now see where your arguments can lead, Tony.'

Blair knew he had lost out. His original point was now hopelessly buried beneath Monica's righteous indignation. The thought again passed through his mind that Burton was using his wife as a stalking horse. If so, it was a very effective double act. It could explain a lot about their strange marriage.

Burton could see the tide running his way and now pushed his advantage home. 'To avoid this kind of loose discussion in the future,' he said, from the chair, 'I propose the following motion.' He had scribbled something down while he was listening. 'That this company, operating as a simple carrier, is concerned only with commercial judgements.'

'Providing it complies with international law,' Blair said.

Burton said he was quite happy to accept that as an amendment and incorporate it in his motion. He now proposed to put it to the vote.

'All those in favour?'

Mason raised his hand. He hated to have to agree with Burton on anything, but was forced to in this case. Blair said he'd like to abstain, but Burton told him he couldn't since his amendment was now part of the motion. He raised his hand limply. He knew Monica would make him pay for it later.

'Kim?' Burton asked.

She raised her hand in acceptance. Monica glanced at her sharply and tightened her lips. The feminine front had collapsed at the first assault.

'Then the motion is passed,' Burton said, and moved on to next business.

They all filed out of Burton's office half an hour later. Monica avoided Blair and stalked off to a meeting of the National Union of Journalists.

She got back to the penthouse after midnight. Burton was still up, studying a company report.

'Charles,' she said icily, 'I have asked a colleague on the *Observer* to find out the details of that arms deal. She thinks it will make a very good story.'

She then stalked off to the bedroom.

Burton hurried after her.

'Monica, we've always had an understanding that you don't put newshounds on to any of my business deals.'

'That's right, Charles,' she said. 'And I've always stuck to it. But now I've changed the rules. All right?'

Since the board meeting had finished early, Blair thought this was as good a time as any to sort Janet out. He drove back to Stanwick village, stopped at the Eagle and went straight up to her room.

She got out of her bath to answer the door. She looked several inches shorter in her bare feet. Her hair was in rats' tails and there was a smear of wet make-up base down her neck. He had her at a disadvantage and she knew it.

'Hullo, Tony! This *is* a surprise. Would you just give me half an hour – I'll see you in the bar.'

But he already had one foot inside the door.

'We'll talk now, and here,' he said. He pushed the door open and walked in.

She always recovered quickly.

'All right,' Janet said cheerfully. 'Carry on talking.'

She went back into the bathroom but left the door ajar. A moment later he saw the bathrobe drop on the floor and heard her get back into the bath. She called out.

'Have you eaten?'

'Yes,' he lied. He had no intention of trying to tackle her in a crowded restaurant.

'Pity, I'm starving. Help yourself to a drink.'

There was a full bottle of scotch on the bedside table. Not yet opened. Odd, he thought. She'd established the other night at table that she didn't drink now. And she had never drunk scotch at any time. He looked at the label. Laophraig. It used to be his favourite malt when they were together. The bottle had been put there for him, so she must have been expecting him at some time. He should have left it unopened, but his thirst got the better of him and he poured himself half a tumbler.

'Water in here,' she called. She knew he always took it half and half.

'I'll take it neat,' he said.

He heard her get out of the bath and turn on a basin tap. A moment later she emerged with a bath towel draped round her and a tumbler of water in her hand. She poured half into his scotch and said, 'I'm so glad you and Paul have hit it off. It's made him very happy.'

'How long are you staying in the area?' Blair asked.

'I don't know,' she said lightly. 'Does it disturb you?'

'It disturbs Paul,' Blair said.

She walked back to the bathroom and carried on the conversation from there. 'You wouldn't understand the bond between us,' she said, adding graciously, 'but I wouldn't expect you to. You never saw him grow up.'

'He's grown up *now*,' Blair said. 'When are you going to let him go?'

He could see her towelling herself through the half-open door and deliberately looked away.

'Everyone is free to do as they wish,' she said, 'including me.'

'How free?' Blair asked.

'I wondered when you were going to ask that,' Janet said. 'Alan has gone to South Africa, he intends to settle there. I do not intend to join him. We parted amicably.'

'Are you going to divorce him?' Blair asked.

'There's no need,' Janet said casually. 'We were never married.'

Blair was stunned. He had automatically assumed that once their own divorce had gone through, Janet had married Alan McLeod.

'You mean you lived together for ten years without ever getting him to the registrar's office!' he said in amazement.

'He wasn't free,' she said. 'Carol never let him go.' She appeared in the doorway from the bathroom in her dressing gown again, but this time far more in possession of herself, talced and scented.

'I thought you knew that,' she went on.

'I never knew a thing. I didn't bother to find out,' Blair admitted.

Paul hadn't mentioned a thing about this to his father, except for the obscure remark about never calling Alan 'Dad'. Blair, presumably, was supposed to read between the lines, just as Janet was now reading his thoughts.

'So you're the only husband I ever had, Tony,' she said. 'And Paul's only father.'

She took a hair drier out of her bedside drawer and switched it on.

It was now impossible to carry on any conversation with her above the hum of the drier.

He reached over and jerked the lead out of the switch-point. 'I said I wanted to talk to you, Janet!'

She shrugged.

'Time,' she said, 'hasn't improved your bad manners.'

'Or your bloody arrogance,' Blair replied angrily. Then stopped himself as he realized they were suddenly starting to quarrel again like husband and wife. He took control of himself, took another drink from the bottle and went to sit down on an easy chair. Janet sat on the bed, then slowly swung her legs up and lay back. She started to breathe deeply, letting her body relax.

'Christ,' Blair said. 'Are you still doing that bloody yoga?'

'It improves the temper,' she said. 'You should try it.' And went on exhaling.

It was time to come to the point.

'If you've come over here hoping I'll support you now your boyfriend's walked out, you can think again, Janet.'

He went on to tell her every penny he had was tied up in the business and would be for some time to come. He said he had no obligations to her or she to him. She had made her own bed and now she could lie in it. She let him ramble on without comment. He glanced across. One massive inhalation in tribute to Zen had caused her gown to fall open a few inches and reveal one breast and a stretch of brown belly. She made no attempt to cover it again. Her eyes were now closed. A fragment of his nightmare dream flashed across his mind. The hotel. The lift. Janet in the lift, naked. Her body pressed against him. He remembered that he hadn't resisted, and was glad to feel her warmth again. This was absurd. Blair was a rational man. Nightmares don't precede events, he argued to himself. Perhaps in Janet's world they might, with her half-boiled mystic rubbish about fate and destiny, but not in his. Or perhaps it wasn't his dream at all, but Janet's dream and he had blundered into it. No, that didn't make sense. It was the bloody whisky. The whisky she had left for him like Eve's apple. He had to get out of here, while she was still asleep. He got to his feet. He was hungry. Whisky on an empty stomach . . . and malt, of course. The Celtic elixir that turned hard Scotsmen into sentimental fools. Malt whisky, he always said, had been invented not by peat-hard clansmen to keep out the Highland cold, but by their subtle witchwives to lure their menfolk into soft seduction. In future he would stick to the blended kerosene the Scots export to America in heather-labelled bottles.

He was halfway to the door when she said, 'If you're up, darling, would you get me my slippers out of the wardrobe, my feet are cold.'

She wasn't asleep.

He should have kept walking to the door, but like Pavlov's dog responding automatically to the whispered command he went to the wardrobe and opened the doors. The rails were heavy with expensive clothes. A blue mink, a short sable jacket for evening wear, silk evening gowns, tailored suits that smelt of Bond Street, leather, mohair, satins and brocade. The bottom was laid out with Italian shoes. Half a dozen pairs, none looked as though they had been worn.

He stood staring at it all for a moment. She watched him, then she said, 'Does that answer your point?'

He turned to face her. She was now half sitting up, her gown still hanging loose. 'Alan did very well out there. It was a large farm. He also had a lot of copper shares. I had a new Mercedes every year, despite the sanctions.'

'Bully for you,' Blair said.

'For all his faults, he was a generous man,' she went on. 'And made a generous settlement.' She smiled. 'You see, I don't really need your support. There's nothing to be afraid of.'

He felt the anger rising in his throat again.

'And you took my remittance money, you bitch!'

It had been part of the settlement. Every month a banker's order from his own hard-earned income went out to Rhodesia for Janet to support their son. Not once had any message come back that she no longer needed it. Over the ten years it must have amounted to something like £30,000 to £40,000.

'That was for Paul,' she said. 'For his education. That was the understanding. I didn't spend a penny of it on myself.'

Now he was white with fury.

'You could have had a new Mercedes every *other* bloody year and sent him to Eton without batting an eyelid,' he shouted.

'I thought you *wanted* to support Paul's schooling,' she said calmly. 'To maintain your sense of fatherhood.'

He crossed over to her, took her by the shoulders and shook her like a wet dog. 'If that money had been in my bank, I wouldn't have had to sell the cottage to raise the money for the business! I couldn't have had to dance to Burton's bloody tune!'

'Rubbish, Tony. You'd have spent every penny of it on drink and air hostesses, and you know that damn well!'

He did know it, if he'd had time to stop to think about it. Without fully realizing it, Blair and his ex-wife had followed a pattern of behaviour so familiar to them both that it had taken on a dynamic of its own. She would needle him with a faint disdain. He would get angry and want to grab her physically, not to hurt her, but to stop her taunting him. His anger, fired now with physical contact, would fuse into lust. Her taunts, laced with the fear of punishment would change her instantly from the verbally dominant to physically passive. He demanded retribution, she felt guilt. Both knew how it would end, but neither could prevent it. Husbands and wives establish patterns and ten years apart will not break them once the sequence is set in motion. Janet would call it fate, Blair would call it folly, but that would come later. He felt her belly, and then her long searching kiss, just as in the dream.

Afterwards, they even repeated the old familiar responses.

Janet said, 'Feel better for the exercise?'

And Blair said, 'Now where had we got to before I was interrupted?'

Soon they fell to arguing again, like husband and wife. Then he got up, dressed and went away like a thief in the night. She lay back and went to sleep without bothering about her yoga.

At about the same time, Monica was lying in bed, restless and alone. She could hear the faint murmur of her husband talking on the telephone in the other room. He had been phoning for more than an hour. She had no idea who to, only that one call followed another and occasionally he would raise his voice as though in frustration or anger. Either the recipients were being woken up from slumber or the calls were overseas to different time zones, since it was now past one o'clock. She knew he was in trouble; she could feel it through the walls, but she had no intention of asking why, or even offering words of comfort. It served him right, she thought. He conducted his affairs with such secrecy that he was not entitled to commiseration when things went wrong.

He was such an amoral bastard she could not imagine why she had ever agreed to marry him. Well, on second thoughts, yes, she could. The wedding had bought her freedom. She thought back to the struggling years on the provincial rag. The awful banalities of the features she had written about local nonentities, the excruciating search for the right cliché that would satisfy the boundless egos of the pompous councillors, the unworthy merchants, the awful opera group and the dull drama societies without actually descending into fawning flattery. Then the thrill of breaking into a national with a freelance article on battery pigs filled with such honest indignation that she had been sure they would reject it. The hectic frenzy of researching the follow-up articles to establish her precarious foothold in the Street. Then the slow disillusion as she learnt that the nationals were only the provincials writ large. That she must still watch her step, give praise where none was due, turn live people with all their complexities into stereotypes for bored copy editors. Keep it simple, keep it trendy, but, above all, give us bright copy.

There were compensations, of course. She now mixed with the wealthy and the famous. She was surprised at first to find that they were often as dull and boring as the small-town worthies from whom she had fled, but their activities were more vivid and had greater import. Yet she knew she was still a hack, though now a better-paid one. Her great ambition was to buy enough time from her routine work to write about the things she really cared for. But life was now more expensive and the tax structure ensured she could never quite make enough to buy more than a few weeks at a time, most of which she would waste unwinding from her labours. At the age of thirty she had taken a long, cool look at her prospects. She would either stay a service writer for life or find herself a patron. The easiest patron to land is a rich husband, so when she found herself interviewing a financial whizzkid called Charles Burton and he had openly offered to take her to bed, she resolved to keep him there on a more permanent basis.

Monica turned on her side in the foetal position. Had she really been all that cold-blooded? No, she wasn't being fair to herself. For a short while she had convinced herself she actually loved this man. She knew now that it wasn't genuine love. She had been infatuated by his air of mystery and the aura that surrounded his activities. But had he ever loved *her*? She now doubted that as well. He had appeared to be in love for the first few months, but perhaps he just loved showing her around. He was uncomfortably in awe of her profession. Being married to a writer must be like being married to a spy. You can never be sure they are not ferreting out your innermost secrets to broadcast to the enemy. Perhaps he got a kick out of that and mistook it for love. But if love involved genuine compassion and concern for others he had failed horrifyingly at the first test. After a year of marriage she decided she needed the experience of pregnancy and the commitment of a child. She flushed all her pills down the loo and waited eagerly for his return from a long business trip to New York. The first night he got back he told her it was too painful for him to make love to her as he had just had a vasectomy in a Manhattan clinic. Vasectomies were the in thing on the eastern seaboard at the time. With the New York Women's Lib movement on the rampage, the Manhattan male was reacting like a scorpion ringed by fire, preferring self-mutilation to surrender. Someone had talked Charles into it in the Algonquin bar.

They had the most dreadful flaming row. How any husband could have gone ahead and done such a thing without even discussing it with his wife was totally beyond Monica's comprehension. He fell back on the lame excuse that he did not want to interfere with her career by risking impregnating her in error, and since she always championed women's rights she should be pleased he had not chained her to the cot during her most creative period. He even had the gall to quote from an article she had once written to this effect, omitting the point she had made in the last paragraph that it was up to the woman to choose. Later she remembered that the sub-editor had cut this paragraph for length, but this did not excuse her husband's atrocious behaviour in taking this irredeemable step without her knowledge. She told him she would have her child anyway, and started an affair within a fortnight with a television critic from a quality Sunday newspaper. But he too proved infertile, so she went back on the pill to await Mr Right. Preferably Mr Right with balls.

Then Blair came into her life.

She had just started to sort Blair out in her mind when she noticed that her husband had stopped telephoning in the next room. A few moments later he came into the bedroom, undressed, showered and came to bed. He was clearly still worried. It showed in his face. He said nothing about the problems he had been phoning about, but she could tell they were still unresolved. After a few minutes he started trying to make love to her. She turned firmly away from him. In her mind's eye she could see the sad eyes of helpless calves being flown to the slaughter. She could hear anguished cries of children crying for their mothers murdered in some distant land by the filthy arms trade her husband was now involved in.

Now she knew why he had become a eunuch, so he could kill without passion.

The following morning, Blair drove Paul in to work in silence. He did not tell the boy he had seen his mother the night before, still less that he had slept with her. But the boy seemed to sense something. He was more cheerful that morning than he had been for days. Once again, the father had nightmare thoughts of conspiracy, but dismissed them. Paul simply seemed to be enjoying his company. He also said he was enjoying the job and had now found a rapport with Kim Hayward. He said she seemed a very nice girl.

On arrival at Red-Air offices, Blair was greeted by a stentorian Aussie shout of greeting. Robertson hurried over to him.

'Tony, are you still looking for a spare motor?'

'A couple, if I can lay my hands on them,' Blair said.

'How far are you prepared to go for them?' Robertson asked.

'Any distance,' Blair said, 'so long as they're cheap and in good nick.'

'Then it's your lucky day, mate. I've just had a call from a mate of mine back home. He flies a Brit from Adelaide up to the Alice. He was just touching down at Oodnabloodydatta when a big red roo hopped out under his undercart. He ended up ripping his belly hold out and now she's a write-off. But he reckons she's got four good motors.'

'Where's Oodnabloodydatta?' Blair asked.

'Halfway up the bloody Birdsville track, mate. Want to take a look at her?'

'Why not?' Blair said. No pilot relished hearing about an accident, but a non-fatal crash leaving four good motors was just what they needed.

'Then I'll call him back and tell him to hold them. You'll have to put your skates on, all the salvage blokes'll be sniffing round there like bloody dingoes.'

A nice long trip to Australia, Blair thought, was just what he needed right now.

6

Blair had got to know the Australians pretty well when he was out in the Far East. He knew from experience you could trust an Aussie with your life, sometimes with your wife, often with your money but never to tell the unvarnished truth about an incident if there was the slightest chance of turning it into an entertaining anecdote. He also knew that when it came to aircraft safety they were red hot, both in the air and on the ground, and the chance of anyone letting a large red kangaroo hop over the perimeter fence and on to a runway with a plane coming in, even in an out-of-the-way spot like Oodnadatta, was pretty remote. So he checked the story out with a friend of his at Qantas. But the essence of the story turned out to be true. There had been a substantiated report of a Britannia landing on its belly, though the cause of the accident was not known until the accident investigators had been over the wreck. But his informant told him that eye-witness reports indicated the damage had been confined to the undercarriage and belly hold and the motors seemed to have escaped largely unscathed. Certainly there had been no fire. Blair felt it was worth going out to look, and discussed it with Mason.

His first instinct was to fly the Red-Air Britannia out there, tramping his way around the world, picking up cargoes en route. But Mason was sceptical. He could certainly take Burton's next arms shipment out as far as Abu Dhabi, but after that there was very little chance of picking up cargo on the Eastern route. Whatever was available was usually snapped up by the long-haul jets from the national airlines. From Hong Kong south to Singapore and Sydney was pretty well locked up by the competitive Far East carriers, and he could hang around for weeks to pick up a few crumbs. If Blair was in a hurry to get to the crashed Brit before all the other vultures, his best plan was to take an engineer and fly out that day on a scheduled passenger line, then, if the motors proved worth buying, arrange for a long-haul carrier to fetch them back to the UK. This would be cheaper than taking their own Brit out of service for a week.

While Kim made the flight arrangements, Blair called Burton to tell him he would be away for a few days. Burton made no objection, in fact, Blair thought he sounded quite pleased. He would need money, cash on the nail if he knew the Aussies. Burton hesitated for a fraction at this, then told him to call him from Australia when he knew the price of the motors and he would arrange it.

Blair hurried back to the flat to pack a bag. Just as he was leaving for Heathrow, Monica called.

'I hear you're off to Australia,' she said over the phone. 'Can I come with you?'

Blair laughed.

'Does your old man want you to keep an eye on me in case I spend too much?'

She sounded offended.

'I'm going off my own bat,' she said sharply. 'I want some background material for an article, but I'm more than happy to travel alone.'

She slammed the phone down on him and he had to ring back and apologize. It was a boring trip out to the Antipodes whichever way you travelled, and a few days away with Monica sounded infinitely more interesting than spending the flight talking shop to Pete, the engineer.

She accepted his apologies with some relief. She didn't want to travel alone either. They met in the departure lounge at Heathrow to board the Qantas jumbo to Sydney via Bahrein and Kuala Lumpur. Not the most entertaining route, but the fastest of the subsonics.

'You don't particularly want to watch the inflight films, do you?' he asked.

'Not wildly,' she said.

'Good, that means we can get some sleep.' He bagged three centre aisle seats up for'ard beyond the screen. The plane was only two-thirds full and he knew no one would be bothered about seat placings after the first nine dreary hours, so he might as well get in first. After half an hour in the air the hostess came over to them.

'Excuse me, sir, but you won't be able to see the films from here,' she said with her special airline dewfresh smile.

'I know,' said Blair, smiling back.

She looked rather nonplussed and retreated.

At Bahrein there was a crew change and another golden blonde from some sunbaked North Sydney beach came over to them with the same smile and the same solicitous comment.

'Why are they all so keen for us to see their movies?' Monica asked finally.

'They're not,' he said. 'These are the seats the cabin staff use for a quiet kip in the small hours, so they try and tempt you away with John Wayne.'

It was nice travelling with someone who knew the ropes, she thought.

Later on, he flashed his BALPA card and took her on to the flight deck. He and the skipper swapped experiences while she watched the sun rise at absurd speed as they hurtled eastwards round the edge of the world.

When they got back to their seats she asked, 'Don't you miss it?'

'Flying the big ones? Not a bit,' he said. 'It's a bloody office job.'

He asked her about the article she planned to write. She said it was a bit vague in her mind at the moment, but she was preparing a series of articles on ecology in the third world.

'Australia's not the third world,' he said. 'It's the lost world.'

She said she hoped to get up to Papua New Guinea.

It all sounded *very* vague. He grinned.

'I think you were just finding an excuse to get away from your husband.'

'That too,' she admitted.

'Then why choose me as a companion? Last time we met, you told me I was just as bad as he was.'

'Neither of you have any sense of ethics,' she said. 'But you're not vicious with it.'

'If he's vicious,' Blair asked, 'why do you stay married to him?'

'Good question,' she said. But made no attempt to answer it.

He suggested they should try to get some sleep.

'How can you sleep when the sun's just risen?'

He told her pilots had to learn to sleep by Greenwich Mean time.

He put his seat back and closed his eyes. After a while she lay across the three seats with her head in his lap.

But he found it hard to sleep. His mind kept wandering to thoughts of Janet. What the hell made him do it? When he walked into her hotel room he knew within minutes that she must have been baiting a trap for him for days. Why hadn't he said what he wanted to say and got out again fast? Because he didn't want to. That was the only answer that made sense. But the marriage had been dead for a decade, how could there possibly be any feeling left between them?

But there must have been something or he could not have made love to her. If you could call it love. He hoped it was no more than a temporary need. But how did he know it was only temporary? Perhaps that's all love ever was – need. If so, where did Monica fit into the picture?

When he had met her in the airport lounge he had felt a tremendous sense of exhilaration, knowing they would be thrown together for a few days. Surely that must be love as well. He ran his fingers through her hair. Did every man need two women, one for domestic comfort the other for best – like suits? The trouble with women was they always forced you to choose. And if you couldn't make your mind up, they'd do it for you. He looked down at Monica's face as she dozed peacefully on his lap. Had she chosen already?

As the jumbo hurtled on into the morning 39,000 feet above the Indian Ocean, Blair wondered how he'd got himself into this. A month ago he had been footloose and fancy free. Now there were two women in his life. Flying men should keep flying. Once they came down to earth they did so at their peril. Earth was women's realm.

Kim Hayward couldn't make up her mind about Paul. She had resented him when he first arrived because he was Blair's son and Blair was the man who had conspired to cheat her boss – or that's how it seemed at the time. Now things seemed to have settled down she found she quite liked the boy. He was always polite and treated her with respect. He was also industrious. That was another quality she admired. In some ways he seemed rather immature, even for his age. This brought out her mothering instinct. He seemed to respond to that. A mother's boy, she decided. At the same time he was clearly in awe of his father, so he didn't quite fit the textbook.

They both worked in the same traffic office since there wasn't room for his desk elsewhere, and she would often glance up to find him gazing at her. She wasn't quite sure whether it was a lascivious look or not and the uncertainty made her feel uncomfortable. She was used to lascivious glances and knew exactly how to respond to them, but Paul's steady gaze seemed a genuinely admiring one. Perhaps he was just an ordinary, old-fashioned nice boy.

Amazing. She thought the breed had died out. Yet he was still his father's son, so there must be a little spark of pure lust somewhere in his make-up. The quiet ones were always the worst.

It didn't take him long to peep quietly out of his shell. His father had left for Australia on the Friday night. It was now Saturday morning. They would keep the office open until the Brit arrived back from the Middle East at around midday. Then Kim would transfer all calls to her own flat. Paul didn't really need to come in at all since the accounts were up to date, but he had. He had clearly been building up to something all morning, but it was almost time to go before he plucked up enough courage to come out with it.

'Kim,' he said cautiously, 'I hope this doesn't sound a rude question, but what do you do with yourself over the weekends?'

'Clean the flat, do the chores, visit my parents,' she said. 'There's always something. Why?'

He swallowed nervously.

'I was wondering if you'd come out with me this afternoon.'

What a gloriously old-fashioned phrase, she thought: 'come out'.

'Come out where?'

'Well,' he said, 'the pictures or something.'

He really was straight out of a 1930s novel. Perhaps that's what they lived on out there in Rhodesia during sanctions, she wondered: 1930s novels.

There was only one cinema within a mile radius and that was nearly always showing 'X' or double 'A' films. Perhaps he wanted an adult to take him in. No, that was an unkind thought. She dismissed it.

'What's on?' she asked instead.

He didn't know of course, and they had to find the local paper. It turned out to be a double bill – 'Confessions of a Topless Masseuse' and 'Emmanuelle at Girton'. He blushed pink and apologized. To put him at his ease she said she'd already seen them. In any case, she said, she had to do some shopping that afternoon. He looked so disappointed she relented.

'You can come round the market with me if you feel like it.'

He said he would like that. He had shopping of his own to do.

That afternoon he trailed round after her pushing her shopping trolley. He bought the few things he needed for his own weekend catering and she advised him on a small lamb joint for his Sunday lunch. On the way back they dropped off at the flat he normally shared with his father because it was en route. He asked her in for a cup of tea and biscuits. She accepted the tea and declined the biscuits. In the informality of small talk she told him a little about her family. She had been brought up in North London of Anglo-Irish parents. Her father had been a small builder and decorator who had tried to expand too rapidly and had gone bankrupt. Since then he had suffered a heart attack and was now an invalid. She had not meant to tell him this much about her background but he seemed genuinely interested.

'How do they live then, your parents?' he asked.

'They get by,' she said.

'You mean you support them.'

'What makes you think that?' she asked in surprise.

He admitted that his father had told him and that he was not at all surprised to hear it. It was just the kind of thing he would have expected from such a marvellous girl. He blushed again when he said it, more so when she laughed.

'I get tax relief for dependent relatives,' she said.

But he knew it wasn't much, since he was already studying the UK tax structure. His admiration for her was growing with every moment that passed. It was becoming slightly embarrassing.

'Is that why you're not married?' he asked cautiously. 'Because you have to look after your parents?'

'I haven't found anyone I particularly want to marry,' she said lightly. 'Why, do you think I'm on the shelf already?'

He denied it hastily. She felt the conversation was starting to get heavy, thanked him for the tea and got up to leave.

'Could I see you again tomorrow?' he asked, bolder now.

She said she always went to church on Sunday mornings.

'In the afternoon, then,' he said. 'We could go for a walk if the weather's fine.'

Since going for a walk was just about the most innocent proposition anyone had made to Kim for years, she found herself agreeing. He looked so delighted that she went away feeling virtuous. Kim Hayward liked making people happy so long as they didn't make too many demands on her in return.

The jumbo touched down at Mascot airport, Sydney, early Sunday morning, Saturday evening UK time. Blair had a few hours' delay before picking up an Ansett internal flight to Adelaide and then on up to Oodnadatta, so told Monica he would like to take her for a quick tour around Sydney. She had never been to Australia before and on the long final leg of the journey down from Kuala Lumpur he briefed her on what she might expect to find. Australians, he said, had a strange love/hate relationship with the British. Whatever impression she may have formed from Australians in London was no real guide to the native Aussie on his own ground. He enjoyed the fruits of the earth and the wealth of a small population crowded on to the seaboards of a vast continent rich in mineral wealth. At the same time he was isolated from the rest of the world and felt cut off from events. This created a defensiveness which the stranger might find puzzling since it was veiled in a native openheartedness. To the north of this rich land with its relatively tiny population lay the teeming millions of starving, war-torn Asia. The Australians were like rich children in a poor neighbourhood, anxious to make friends but deeply suspicious that their neighbours regarded them with envy and must be concealing an awful animosity towards them behind polite smiles. They feared pretence in even the most innocent remark. They would try to pre-empt hostility by brutal frankness, even when there was no hostility intended. At the same time they genuinely wanted to know how they appeared in the eyes of others.

Blair laid a small bet with Monica that within half an hour of leaving the airport, some complete stranger would ask her what she thought of Australia. It was the great trick question. If she found the slightest criticism she would be regarded as a typical whingeing Pom. If she praised it she would be thought a typical two-faced bloody Pom. There was no way you could win.

They were only five minutes out of Mascot when it happened. The young taxi driver turned to Blair and said, 'Well, mate, what do you think of Australia?'

'It's a bloody great shithouse,' said Blair without a moment's pause. 'All beer and bullshit.'

'Then what did you come here for?' said the Aussie without rancour.

'Couldn't think of anything better to do,' said Blair.

The driver glanced back towards Monica.

'I suppose he's been telling you we're all descended from cons, eh?'

'No,' said Blair. 'I told her you're all descended from prison warders.'

The driver laughed.

'Not in New South Wales, mate. All those ratbags are in Canberra.'

They got on fine after that. He decided they were a couple of good blokes and were entitled to a running commentary on the places they passed through as they did their tour of the city. At times it sounded like a street map of London: Paddington, Oxford Street, Regent Street, Kings Cross, Hyde Park and Haymarket. It was a strange sensation, as though they had travelled to the far side of the world and arrived back home. Then they would suddenly hit an aboriginal name like Woolloomooloo Street or Bennelong Point. They stopped at Bennelong to look at the opera house. Monica gazed at the famous building with its incredible interlocking concrete shells spread up into the air like sails in the wind.

'Nuns playing rugby,' said the taxi driver.

Monica laughed. It did look like that from a distance, heads down, humpbacked, skirts in the air.

After that she said she would like to go to Bondi Beach.

'Forget it,' said the driver, 'it's a bloody open sewer. If you want a decent beach, you have to get up north of Dee Why to Mona Vale, Newport or Palm Beach.' But they didn't have time for anything more than a quick trip over the Harbour Bridge to North Sydney and Cremorne. Monica thought it was the most beautiful single-span bridge in the world.

'It's a bloody coathanger,' said the driver. But he was obviously proud of his city.

'You should see it at night,' Blair told her. 'It's breathtaking.'

But they had to move on. He promised her a night in Sydney when they got back.

Then he remembered she was supposed to be here on her own mission.

'Do you want to come on with me to the outback?' he asked.

'Is it worth a visit?'

'It's an experience you'll never forget,' Blair told her.

She didn't need asking a second time. She seemed to have forgotten all about her articles.

They joined up with Pete, the engineer, who had come out on a later plane, and headed for Adelaide. From there they picked up a light plane bound for Alice Springs via Leigh Creek and their destination, Oodnadatta. Flying at a much lower ceiling than the jets, he was able to show her the sheer magnificence of the South Australian landscape. North over the beautiful Barossa Valley where nineteenth-century German settlers had imported the Shiraz and Hermitage grapes to plant their own vineyards and built neat little homesteads that looked as though they had been brought, stone by stone, from the banks of the Saar. Then up over the mountains of the magnificent Flinders Ranges, that rose gently peak by peak from the south to suddenly fall away like a cliff edge to flat scrub lands and vast areas of salt pan. He showed her Wilpena Pound from the air, a ring of cliff-like mountains white at the top, reddish brown at the base and set in a bed of purple shale. With only one tiny road entering it, the hidden valley inside had once been the perfect hideout for cattle rustlers. From Leigh Creek on they were flying over the real outback, hundreds of miles of powder dry desert scattered with saltbush and loose rock called gibber. This was the start of the infamous Birdsville track where the single narrow gauge railway to Alice Springs had replaced the old camel trains. He showed her the old railhead town of Maree far below, abandoned now and virtually given over to the aborigines who had turned it into a shanty town. It glittered in the sun, the old sheds painted silver.

'The last time I was up this way,' Blair said, 'there was a story that when the aborigines moved in they found a warehouse full of aluminium paint left by the railhead and painted everything in sight.'

'I'd like to meet some aborigines,' she said.

'Then hire a car and take a run down there while I'm seeing to the motors,' Blair said. 'But I'm told that half of them aren't true aborigines, they interbred with the Afghans.'

'What on earth were Afghans doing there?'

He explained that when the Birdsville had first been opened up, an Indian army officer had the bright idea of importing camels from Afghanistan to take packloads up to Alice, he had also imported their Afghan drivers. Later, when the railway took over, they had settled and their camels had run wild. There were still wild camels wandering around the area, the descendants of the original pack animals. The Afghan drivers had intermarried to produce an aborigine with a lighter skin and North Indian bone structure.

He was so full of fascinating stories that they hardly noticed the plane was now coming down to land.

Oodnadatta was little more than a cluster of houses and sheds in the middle of nowhere. The airstrip looked tiny. On the perimeter they could see the crashed Britannia lying on its belly. It looked like a stranded whale. Although part of the wingtip had broken away and two sets of props sheared off, the prospects looked good for salvage. There were already two or three open trucks nosed into its side like piglets at a sow. Blair and his engineer weren't the first scavengers on the scene. Within a week it would be picked as clean as a carcass in the sun.

Charles Burton heaved a sigh of relief when his wife went away. Normally she didn't distract him from his work, but when there was a crisis on he preferred to be alone so he could think things out. By himself in the penthouse he could get mentally stripped for action. Fast action was needed now. The first signs that his financial affairs were starting to get out of control had come while she was off on her Ximbali trip. All his various companies were interlocked in one way or another. This was fine so long as the majority of them were keeping afloat, for they could support the weaker links in the chain. He sometimes thought of his companies as a line of buckets, none of which was more than a third full. But so long as he could tip the contents of two of the buckets rapidly into the third, he could show a full one to anyone who came prying. The moment they started investigating the first bucket he would hastily tip it all back again. But the levels were now all too low for him to expect to get away with this juggling act much longer. He had borrowed heavily over the past year from a merchant bank, but it was a short-term loan now due for repayment. Despite the lifestyle he maintained, Charles Burton was not a wealthy man, simply a nimble man with wealth passing through his hands. It was now slipping through his fingers.

When his wife had fetched him Tony Blair on a plate and he had learnt the cash-flow potential of a small cargo operation, it had come as a gift from the gods. Burton had been thinking for some time of moving into the lucrative world arms trade and had already been in contact with an international arms dealer called Nick Varos. The obvious advantage of the arms trade was that the dealers dealt in cash and into overseas tax havens. Varos had been interested in rocket-firing equipment being phased out by the Fleet Air Arm, but the UK Ministry of Defence would only allow it to go to countries regarded by them as friendly to the West, lest it should end up behind the Iron Curtain. Burton's original intention had been simply to buy it from the Fleet Air Arm on a guarantee that its final destination was the Middle East, sell it to Varos and take his cut. But by acquiring Red-Air he could get a much bigger finger in the pie – he could handle the shipping of it as well. So the two strands had come together at just the right time. So far, so good. Providing he could keep Monica happy. She clearly wanted to have an affair with Blair. Fine, that should keep her occupied for a bit. It also meant he had a hold on Blair if the man should start getting difficult. Providing, of course, he could keep a hold on his wife. And that's where the danger lay.

Monica, he thought, really was a tiresome woman. He

had given her everything she needed. Security, money, a life of comparative luxury and the freedom to take lovers. He had always regarded her wishy-washy liberal ideas with mild amusement. It even gave him a perverse pleasure to hear her castigate his business colleagues at social functions for their naked capitalist greed. This gave *him* a certain cachet – the man who could afford the luxury of a non-conformist wife. And it was also useful on occasions. If someone was close to pinning Burton down, Monica could usually be relied on to divert attention from him with an outburst of moral indignation if he pressed the right nerve. Who would suspect him of nefarious dealings with such a highly principled wife to act as watchdog?

He smiled to himself as he thought of the crucial meeting with his merchant bankers a few months back. They were on the point of accusing him of milking funds out of one of his companies through an account in Cape Town when she had unleashed a ferocious attack on the surprised bankers for dealing with the South Africans and thus supporting apartheid. By the time she had finished with them, he had slipped off the hook. She had done it again at the last board meeting of Red-Air when Blair was trying to nail him over the destination of the arms shipment. But the ploy that pleased him most was her outburst on women's rights at the initial meeting; this had allowed him to slip Kim Hayward on the board without him even having to suggest it. She was not to know that Kim was his creature.

He often wondered whether Monica realized she was being manipulated. She was a highly intelligent lady and could easily work it out for herself if she tried. But the supreme value of moral indignation is that it swamps any attempt at self-reasoning. While she was wallowing in moral outrage, he could plan his next half-dozen ice-cold moves. Or so it had always worked in the past. He now had an uneasy feeling he had overplayed his hand over the arms deal. He had upset her so much she had put a news hound on to him. She had never done that before, and it showed that his hold over her was weakening – either that or she was getting cunning. Whatever the reason it was the first sign of active disloyalty, and that was going too far.

He had tried to warn Varos – that was the night he had spent telephoning – but couldn't trace him. Instead he had left messages with various contacts that he was going to speed up deliveries of the arms shipments before the press stirred things up. So that was the first practical step to be getting on with.

Next he phoned the rear-admiral to arrange for the remainder of the arms shipment to be sent urgently by road to Red-Air's cargo sheds. The customer, he said, was in a hurry. He then called his chauffeur to drive him down to Stanwick.

When Kim Hayward got back to her flat after tea and sympathy from Paul Blair, Burton's car was waiting outside. She let him in without a word, as she had done several times before.

The ground temperature at Oodnadatta was 110 degrees in the shade. There wasn't a lot of shade. Monica said that if the body temperature was that high, you'd be dead. So why wasn't everybody dead?

'Because they're not fool enough to stand around in it,' Blair said, and dragged her off to the tiny airport bar for a long glass of frozen gas topped up with a liquid smelling faintly of beer.

All heads turned as she came in. For a moment she thought they were going to refuse to serve women, but the teak-brown faces of the men were simply giving her the normal outback body scan. Later on, when they found the energy, they would look at her face.

Blair found the owner of the airline leaning up against

the bar talking to two inspectors from the Australian Accident Investigation Board. He was a pilot operator like himself, and it was his only plane. His name was Morphett. He was six feet four tall and came from Adelaide. Blair had no need to introduce himself.

'Tony Blair?' Morphett said, holding out a huge hand. 'Heard you were on your way. Pleased to meet you.'

'That's some bush telegraph you've got here,' Blair grinned.

'Is that your missis?' Morphett asked, his eyes travelling slowly up from her feet.

Blair introduced her as a fellow director.

'Pleased to meet you, Monica,' said the giant. 'What d'you think of Australia?'

'It's hot,' said Monica.

'That's right,' said Morphett.

The answer seemed to satisfy him. He ignored her after that.

After a few more pleasantries and several more beers, they got down to business.

'How many engines are still fit?' Blair asked.

'A couple may need a bit of patching up,' said Morphett airily, 'but the other two are beauties.'

'What exactly happened?' Blair asked.

'Bloody freak dust-storm,' Morphett said. 'Blew up after I was committed to land. I hit the lip of the runway, sheered off the port main landing wheel, tipped up and broke her back.'

'Bit of a short runway to try landing a Brit, wasn't it?' Blair said.

'Had no choice, mate,' said Morphett. 'I couldn't get in at the Alice and didn't have enough fuel to make it back to Adelaide.'

'How much do you want for the two good engines?'

'There's a couple of Chinese down from Singapore offered me a quarter of a million dollars already. Can you top that?' Morphett asked hopefully.

'I've got to get them out of this Godforsaken spot,' Blair said. 'That's going to cost a bit.'

Monica had been wondering how they'd manage that ever since she arrived, but Morphett had a typical Aussie answer.

'Mate of mine runs a cattle truck, he'll shift 'em down the Birdsville for you,' he said.

But Blair knew it wouldn't be that easy.

'When could I look them over?'

'As soon as these two buggers have finished sniffing around,' Morphett said, indicating the accident inspectors beside him.

'Give us a week or ten days,' said the senior of the two inspectors. 'Not in a rush are you?'

Blair said if it took that long, the deal was off.

Morphett looked anxiously at the accident men. 'No need for you blokes to make a meal of it,' he said. 'No one got hurt.'

They said they had to make out a full report, even so.

'But if you know the cause of the accident,' Monica asked, 'why does it need an investigation?'

One of the investigators explained that every accident to an aircraft, however minor, had to be thoroughly examined in case it involved a failure of any part of the aircraft structure. This information was invaluable to other carriers throughout the world flying the same kind of plane.

'Bullshit,' said Morphett. 'These blokes have got nothing better to do.'

But they all seemed to take it in good part and a few beers later it was agreed that Blair's engineer could test the motors the following morning, but no one could take them away until the investigators had cleared them.

It was now clear that they were going to be stuck there for two or three days, so Blair hired a car to show Monica the outback.

As he had promised her, it proved an experience she was not going to forget for the rest of her life. The first thing that struck her was the extraordinary precautions everyone took beneath the Australian veneer of casual indifference. Before setting out, Blair had to check in with the local police to state his destination and assure them that he had enough water on board the car in case he broke down. They checked his spares, made sure he had a spade and towrope and a full tank of petrol. At his stated arrival point he would check in again with the police to make sure he had got there safely. They gave him a route map and warned him to stay with it.

She laughed at this. 'I've spent a fortnight in the African jungle,' she told the Aussie sergeant.

The sergeant told her that Africa was bloody civilized compared with the Australian outback.

A few hours later, as the dirt road gradually declined into a rutted track several feet deep in dust in places, and the sun blazed down mercilessly overhead, she saw the point. For the whole of the rest of that day they passed only two other vehicles. Both stopped, and the drivers checked with each other that they had no problems, and there were no difficulties ahead. They slept in the open that night on the shores of Lake Eyre – a waterless saltpan that seemed to stretch to infinity. The night was even more extraordinary. The whole canopy of sky seemed to close down on them, the stars of the Southern Cross glittering so brightly she felt she could reach out and touch them. The silence was stunning. Whatever wildlife existed in this arid saltbush desert seemed to have disappeared into a soundless void. She felt she had never known such total peace. The night hours drifted away into a dreamless sleep where time and space merged into one.

Suddenly she was wide awake, the sun was warm on her face. She was also alone. She got quickly to her feet and looked around. Blair's sleeping bag lay beside hers, crumpled and empty. She looked towards the spot where they had parked the car the previous night. It was gone. She was seized by a moment of panic. Fifty yards away was a dried-up creek bed with a clump of silver gum trees growing from the bank. She ran towards it, shouting his name. There was no answer.

As she reached the creek bed she sensed that something had changed. She looked up at the silver gums, and stopped in amazement. The night before they had been withered and dry, their branches reaching out against the sky like deadman's fingers. Now they were ablaze with crimson. Each branch seemed to be laden with bright red fruit. Something strange and terrifying had happened overnight. Or had it been just one night? Perhaps a whole season had passed while she had slept through some timeless limbo. She blinked to make sure she was awake and looked again. The crimson-laden trees now held a mystic beauty. Cautiously she walked towards them. She stepped on a dry twig that snapped like a rifle shot in the still air. A moment later the trees exploded into a whirling vortex of colour and the air was full of the frantic rustle of wings, flailing and beating like a sudden storm. The great red canopy rose above the silver gums, turned dark and scattered into fragments.

'Galahs,' said a voice from somewhere below the level of the creek bed. She ran towards the voice, knowing as she did so that it was not Blair's voice. But it was a human sound and somewhere there must be a human being in all this strange emptiness.

She did not see him at first, only the shadow of him. As her eyes adjusted to the intense contrast of shade she slowly made out a short, broad, shabbily dressed figure squatting on the ground beside a silver gum. He wore a pair of black, heavy serge trousers held up with string, faded blue and white plimsolls with holes in the toes, a tattered Fair Isle jersey with a V-neck and a short gaberdine car coat with a fur-trimmed collar. His face was broad, black and pitted. His hair silvery white, his flaring nostrils seemed to merge into his cheeks. But it was his eyes that held her. The pupils were as black as his skin and seemed bottomless.

'G'day,' he said, and when he smiled there were only two yellow stumps of teeth in his huge mouth.

'Good day,' she said, and nodded a salutation.

'Did they scare yer?' he asked in a broad Australian accent.

'Yes,' she said. 'For a moment.'

'Jis bloody parrots,' he said amiably. 'Galah parrots. Roost up at night in the trees.'

'They're beautiful,' she said.

'Yeah,' said the aborigine. 'Bloody menace.'

'Have you seen . . .' she began. Then, because it was simpler, 'my husband?' Even as she said it she found the word sprang easily to her lips.

'Yeah,' he said, after a moment's thought. 'He's with the missis.'

'Whose missis?' she asked, trying not to sound indignant.

'My missis,' said the aborigine, then started to laugh.

She had never seen a laugh quite like it. It started deep in the chest, then seemed to work its way through his frame until his whole body was quivering and he had to hug himself to bring the tremor to a stop. For a moment she thought he was going to roll on the ground like a porcupine. She felt she had to laugh with him, if only to be polite. Then she found her own laugh taking over her body, just as it had the aborigine. It was a mixture of relief from the nervous tension of the past few minutes and genuine amusement at the sheer absurdity of it all. He waited politely for her to stop as though this was a natural courtesy all human beings should extend to each other – never to interrupt the joy of self-amusement. Then he clambered slowly to his feet and started to pad away up the creek bed. After a few yards he turned and beckoned to her. She followed him until they reached a clump of mulga bushes. From somewhere beyond them was a curl of white smoke. She pushed her way through the mulga and looked around. At first she thought she was in a corporation rubbish tip, though what it was doing in the middle of nowhere she could not imagine. The area was littered with old cans, bottles, empty cartons, cardboard boxes, car tyres and the stripped chassis of a huge truck. Scattered amongst the litter was what appeared to be little mounds of spindrift.

Her guide picked his way lightly through the refuse and suddenly disappeared into one of the mounds like a rabbit in a burrow. A moment later figures began to emerge from the ground: a short round woman dressed in a torn yellow cardigan and tartan skirt that scraped the ground, two or three thin youths in torn jeans and bright red T-shirts and tiny black children that seemed to be sprouting from the spindrift like little purple aubergines. They all stood quite still, watching her curiously as she walked towards them. She smiled, and they smiled back, but made no move.

Suddenly, through the smoke, like a pantomime genie, Blair emerged. He was stripped to the waist and covered in black wood ash.

'Come and join us for breakfast,' he called.

Breakfast amongst the aborigine family was a gastronomic experience. Stewed black tea boiled up in half an old petrol can, a rusting tin of pineapple slices that bore a faded label warning the customer they should have been consumed ten years ago and some burnt embers that Blair swore was kangaroo meat but Monica suspected was catfood. Later she was to discover this was their Sunday lunch and they had sacrificed it in honour of their visitors. Conversation was largely limited to a series of smiles and hand gestures. Although the old man who had acted as her guide spoke English and the others clearly understood it, no one seemed to want to waste good eating time with conversation. At the same time they seemed to be communicating quite fluently with each other by means of small movements of the hands and subtly inclined head gestures. Monica learnt that they were on their way down from the aborigine reserves in the Musgrave Ranges to look for work. But they didn't seem to be in a hurry as they must have been on this site for months, judging by the surrounding litter.

Later, when it was time to leave, Monica drew Blair aside and said she thought they should offer to pay for the meal as they seemed so poor. Blair said they would be more than happy with half a dozen cans of beer. He had some in the boot of the car. Then she remembered.

'Where *is* the car, anyway?'

'They hid it,' Blair said.

He led her over to one of the larger clumps of spindrift, and saw that the car was carefully disguised beneath it.

'What for?'

'Fun,' said Blair. 'Mind you, if I hadn't discovered them, they might just have hoped we'd give it up as lost and hitch a lift back.'

They drove off with the aborigine kids, now over their shyness, hanging on to the back, laughing and shouting until they dropped off one by one.

Later she said, 'This morning, when I woke up, I thought you'd abandoned me.'

'As if I would,' Blair said.

'You nearly did that time at Ximbali,' she reminded him.

'I didn't know you then,' he said.

She watched his face carefully as he wrestled with the steering wheel down the dry creek bed.

'Didn't you want to wake up with me this morning?' she asked finally.

'It was your first morning in the outback,' he said. 'I thought you'd prefer to wake alone. An experience like that shoudn't be spoilt by conversation.' It was at that moment, in the middle of an arid wilderness on the shores of a dried-up lake 12,000 miles from home that Monica knew she loved this man and wanted to keep him.

Charles Burton declined the chair Kim offered him. He preferred to give instructions standing up, or pacing around her small sitting room.

'I want to get the entire war-surplus shipment away over the next three days,' he said. 'Can that be done?'

'Only by keeping the aircraft flying round the clock,' she said.

'Good. Then let's do that,' Burton said.

'We can't,' she said. 'We'd need three complete crews and with Captain Blair and his spanner away, we only have two.'

'Then we sign up a spare crew. No problem,' Burton said.

'It's Captain Blair's job to take on crews,' Kim said.

'Can't you do it off your own bat?'

'You can't ask me to go over his head. Besides, crewing up that old plane isn't easy. Even Blair finds it hard to talk pilots into it. What chance would I have?' she asked.

'Mason must know where to find pilots in a hurry,' Burton said.

'Then you'd better go to him, Mr Burton,' Kim said coldly. 'I don't have the authority.'

'You're a director of the company,' Burton snapped. 'You and I have the authority to take these decisions when the others are away. We also have the authority to instruct Captain Mason to do as we ask. So will you please make the necessary arrangements.'

She bit her lip, trying to control her temper.

'Nothing can be done until Monday morning,' she said. 'Apart from lining up the extra crew, we have to get route clearances.'

'Then start tonight,' Burton said. 'I want that first flight away at dawn tomorrow morning.'

'Tomorrow's Sunday,' she said.

'Then you'll have to miss church for once, won't you?' Burton said. She could have defied him. She could have raised half a dozen objections over technical procedure that he would know nothing about, but she knew there was no point. Charles Burton was used to having his own way.

'All right,' she said finally. 'I'll do the best I can, though it's very short notice and I can't promise anything.'

'Good,' Burton said abruptly. 'I knew I could rely on you, Kim.'

'There are two conditions,' she said.

He raised an eyebrow. The girl was starting to lay down her own terms now.

'Firstly,' she went on, 'you have to square it with Ray Mason, not me.'

'Does he have to know about it yet?' Burton asked.

'Yes. That plane only landed a few hours ago. He has to have it checked out and passed fit to fly in the morning,' she said.

'All right,' Burton said. 'I want to talk to him anyway. What's your second condition?'

'That you tell me why you're in such a hurry, Mr Burton. And I want the truth.'

'I think your directorship has gone to your head, Miss Hayward,' Burton said icily.

'It gives me the right to ask questions like that and expect an answer,' she said, facing up to him.

Burton decided on a half-truth. He told her that the shipments could be stopped by bad publicity and it could break at any time. He did not tell her his own wife had put the boot in, that was none of Kim's business. But Kim wasn't prepared to let it go at that.

'I don't know what this bad publicity might reveal, Mr Burton,' she said, 'but if it proves this company has broken any laws, national or international, we could be in trouble. Captain Mason could lose his licence and Red-Air would be out of business.'

Burton shrugged. He now seemed quite amiable again. Even managed a smile. 'I may bend laws occasionally, Kim,' he said. 'But I'm always careful never to break them. And if anyone suggests it in public I'll sue.'

He started to move to the door. She stepped in front of him.

'I don't think you care,' she said. 'Once this shipment is away, you don't give a damn what happens to Red-Air, do you?'

'Do you really think I would throw away such a valuable asset?' he asked mildly.

'No,' said Kim. 'But you may have plans to capitalize on it.'

'Any plans that may evolve,' Burton said carefully, 'would certainly involve you and you wouldn't be the worse for it. So you have no need to worry.'

Then, abruptly, he changed the subject.

'How's your father?' he asked.

'Dying slowly,' she said.

'Is there anything I can do?' He sounded sincere and she knew that, in this respect, he was.

'No,' she said, softening. 'You've done enough.'

When he left her flat, Burton went back in his car, picked up the telephone and dialled Mason's number. It was Audrey who answered. Burton immediately switched on the charm.

'Mrs Mason, we've never actually met. This is Charles Burton speaking.'

'Just hold on a minute, Mr Burton, I'll see if Ray's free.' She sounded cool.

'Actually,' Burton said hastily down the phone, 'it's you I wanted to speak to.'

She listened in silence as he explained that he found himself in the area and unexpectedly free due to a cancelled appointment. He had been meaning to invite them both to dinner and now seemed the perfect opportunity. Would it be at all possible later on that evening? He sounded, Audrey thought as she took the call on her kitchen extension, as though butter wouldn't melt in his mouth.

She explained that she was already preparing their own dinner and they had a guest. But he sounded so genuinely disappointed that she began to have second thoughts. Maybe it would be a good idea to meet this man she had heard so much about. She could give him a piece of her mind.

'Unless, of course,' she added cautiously, 'you'd like to join *us*.'

Burton thanked her profusely, said he would be round in half an hour and hung up. How useful, he thought, that they had a guest. Mason would be obliged to behave himself. He told his driver to take him to the Eagle where he knew they kept a reasonable wine cellar.

When Audrey put her end of the phone down, she began to wonder if she'd made a mistake. Ray had been looking forward to a nice evening's gossip about old times. But it was too late now. She went into the sitting room where he was entertaining the guest. Predictably, he blew his top.

'You've invited that bastard to dinner! You must be bloody mad!' he shouted.

'I thought it was time I met this ogre,' Audrey said.

'Me too,' said Janet Blair.

7

Just about the time that Blair and Monica were squatting down amongst the detritus of the aborigines to share their dawn breakfast of pineapple slices and catfood, on the dark side of the earth Audrey was preparing a duck à l'orange for Saturday-evening dinner. She was quite glad there would now be four at table instead of three. It was much easier to cut a duck into quarters. She only hoped there would be enough pudding to go round. As she prepared the orange sauce she mentally rehearsed what she would say to that slick bugger Burton if he started pushing her Ray around again. A Yorkshire girl of solid Doncaster mining stock, she based her philosophy on two sound principles: it was a woman's job to stand by her husband, and never trust anyone born south of the Humber. She was just casting around in her memory for a few nice pithy Yorkshire phrases when the doorbell chimed. She hoped Ray would answer it as she couldn't leave the kitchen, but when it chimed a second time it was obvious he wasn't going to bother. Too busy making sheep's eyes at Janet Blair in the sitting room, she supposed. She never could quite work out if there had ever been anything between those two all those years back. On balance she thought not. Ray was too sexually idle to have a woman on the side, except for a good gossip. But it didn't stop him making passes to annoy her. The doorbell had chimed a third time before she had put the saucepan aside, taken off her pinny and reached the hall. Impatient bugger, she thought. Typical Southerner.

She opened the door to find not one man in the porch,

but two. A short smooth one in a smart chalk-striped suit and a tall lanky one in a grey uniform with a peaked cap carrying two bottles wrapped in tissue paper and a large bunch of flowers. Bloody heck, she thought, am I supposed to feed his footman as well? But she needn't have worried. Burton took the goodies from the peaked cap and dismissed him. She presumed he would have to make do with the local chip shop. She accepted the flowers with a curt word of thanks and ushered Burton into the sitting room with his bottles.

Charles Burton had spent most of his adult life perfecting the social graces. Not because he believed they had any intrinsic value, but because he knew them to be an instrument of power. No more so than when dealing with his financial inferiors, and most particularly when women were present. Within five minutes of arrival he was chatting easily with Janet and neatly parrying Mason's gruff responses with polite smiles. Janet had been an unexpected surprise and he was not slow to take advantage of it. Previously he had known very little about Blair's past life because it hadn't interested him. But it did now. In fact, it opened up a whole new ball game. By the time they were seated at table, Burton reckoned he had Janet worked out. She was sharp, subtle, self-seeking and clearly intent on getting her ex-husband back under her wing. She might talk a lot of tommy rot about fate and destiny, but that was probably her party conversation piece. Her main value to him was as valuable counterweight to Monica. Now that, he thought, could be fascinating. Playing games with triangles could get boring after a while, a square dance was a far greater challenge to the intellect.

Janet, for her part, was also making her assessment. Burton, she guessed, was either asexual or bisexual. He never once let his eyes wander over her body, concentrating entirely on her face. His eyes were cold and very blue, but she suspected he wore tinted contact lenses as they didn't match his hair colour or skin pigment. He was obviously intuitive and lightning quick in catching mood changes in others. A planner and a plotter who moved like a silverfish. She liked him instinctively, not as a man, but as a worthy opponent. Poor Tony, she felt, with his rude honesty and tramline patterns of thought, could be no match for such a man. Tony needed her protection far more than he realized.

Audrey might have detected the play between the two, but she was too busy serving the duck. Mason missed it completely. He was just wondering when Burton was going to reveal the reason for his surprise call.

It came as they were halfway through the second course and Burton was congratulating Audrey on her cuisine. Without a pause for breath he was suddenly into business.

'I don't imagine that Britannia can last much longer,' he said to Mason. 'What do you think we should replace it with, a CL 44?'

The CL 44 was the stretched version of the Britannia, and since it carried an extra nine tons of payload, was a more economic aircraft.

'You wouldn't get much change out of six hundred thousand quid for a forty-four,' Mason said. 'Have you got that kind of money?'

'It could be raised,' Burton said casually.

Audrey thought this was her chance to score a point on behalf of her husband.

'If it's that easy to raise money, Mr Burton,' she said tartly, 'why didn't you do it before, instead of buying Ray out for next to nothing?'

Mason shot her a warning glance. She was trying to help, but he wished she'd keep out of it.

But Burton seemed to take no offence. He explained courteously that whereas one could always raise money on a going concern, it was impossible if a business was near liquidation.

'It wasn't Ray's fault,' she said stoutly. 'People didn't pay their debts.'

'Go and get the pudding,' said Mason. He wanted to think out Burton's latest ploy. If Burton was now thinking of scrapping the Brit and replacing it with another aircraft, his own job was in the balance. So long as they flew that Britannia on Mason's own operating certificate, he had a foothold in Red-Air. The moment the Brit was scrapped, he would be scrapped with it. He had to forestall the move.

'What makes you think the CAA are going to give you a certificate to fly a CL 44?' he asked.

'I'm thinking ahead, Ray,' Burton said amiably. 'By that time I think we shall have proved to the authority we are a reliable carrier. Don't you?'

'Yeah,' Mason said acidly, 'with my help.'

'Both Blair and I recognize your help has been invaluable,' Burton said smoothly. 'And we both hope you will stay with us as the company expands.'

Lying bastard, thought Mason, but he couldn't very well say so in front of Janet.

'So he should,' Audrey said as she collected the dirty plates. 'And I think he's entitled to a lot more shares than that, as well.'

'Audrey,' said Mason for the second time, 'get the pudding.'

Janet got up to help Audrey carry the dishes into the kitchen, which left the two men alone for a few minutes. It was Mason's chance to talk frankly.

'Now listen, mate,' he began.

Burton hated being called 'mate'.

'Charles,' he said.

'Now listen, *Charles*,' Mason said, making it sound like an expletive, 'you haven't even got your toes wet in this business yet. It's getting dicier every year as the cost of fuel goes through the roof. If you start challenging the big operators, they'll crush you. The only chance we've got of surviving is to stay small and live off the payloads they find uneconomic to carry. There'll always be plenty of them around.'

'That policy didn't do *you* much good, did it?' Burton said blandly.

'I was unlucky. You caught me at a bad moment,' Mason said. But he knew it sounded lame.

Burton could have cut him to shreds on that remark alone. He could have told Mason that bad luck was the excuse every small man with limited ambitions made for his own failings; that Mason's tiny shopkeeper mind was as out of date in the modern world of high finance as the horse and cart. But that was not the purpose of the evening's exercise. He had a more limited objective. He appeared to ponder Mason's words for a moment as though he was taking them seriously.

'All right, Ray,' he said at last. 'You may have a point. We'll keep the Britannia for as long as we can, but at the moment it isn't paying its way. We have to work together to ensure faster turnarounds and longer periods in the air earning money.'

'I wouldn't disagree with that,' Mason said. It was the least he could settle for.

'Fine,' said Burton. 'I'd like that plane shuttling to and fro to the Middle East for the next three days and nights. Starting at dawn tomorrow.'

By the time Audrey and Janet came back into the dining room with the baked Alaska, Mason was agreeing to work through the night to make sure the aircraft was ready.

It was easy, thought Burton, dealing with men like Mason. All you had to do was gently threaten them with extinction and they'd jump through hoops for you.

'Sucker,' said Audrey to her husband when Burton and Janet had left soon after. 'Why don't you stand up for yourself?'

'I did!' protested her husband.

'You wouldn't say boo to a goose,' she said scornfully.

Burton had offered Janet a lift back to the Eagle. On the way they discussed Paul. Burton said he seemed a bright and conscientious lad.

'He works well under supervision,' she said pointedly.

Burton smiled. 'I'll keep an eye on him,' he said.

She had visions of her son making a meteoric rise until he was chief accountant to the Burton Enterprises. What a useful evening it had been.

Burton thought so too. But there was still a lot to be done before the runaway lovers returned from Down Under.

It was two days before Pete, Blair's engineer, could get at the engines of the crashed Brit. He tested them *in situ* and after an argument with the accident inspectors, finally got the clearance to have them lifted out. He checked the logs and found they each had 6000 hours left to run on the certificate. It didn't seem a bad buy if the price was right.

Blair and Monica were now back after their outback trip. He had taken her back via Cooper Pedy where the opal miners lived like moles underground and the surface temperature could run as high as 140 degrees. They had driven part of the way back stark naked since they met nothing but incurious kangaroos en route. She felt happy, relaxed and totally dehydrated. While she topped up her parched body in the airport bar, Blair went to argue money with Morphett. He had no intention of paying a quarter of a million Australian dollars for the two engines and hoped to start beating him down. But by this time Morphett had decided on a new sales technique. He claimed that there was now so much interest in the Britannia for spare parts that the only fair way of dealing with it was to hold an auction.

Blair was now in a spot. He had hoped to get away with putting down a substantial deposit and sending the balance to Morphett when he got back to the UK. Now he would have to find it all cash on the nail, and he couldn't be sure how much he would have to find. He had already cabled Burton to warn him of the likely price before he left with Monica on the outback tour, but there was no reply waiting for him. He now decided to telephone him and booked a call through via Adelaide. When he finally got through to the penthouse number he was in for a shock.

'The price is ridiculous,' Burton said down the long-distance phone. 'The company can't afford anything like a quarter of a million dollars.'

'It may run higher than that,' Blair said.

'Then forget it,' Burton snapped.

'Now wait a minute, Charles, you knew roughly what engines would cost before we left. You said you could find it. Why the hell else do you think Monica and I came out here?'

'To give you both an excuse to sleep together, I assumed,' Burton said coldly. 'Was I wrong?'

There was a pause at Blair's end. This was a hell of a time to discuss that subject, over 12,000 miles and bouncing Monica's infidelities off a communications satellite. The local operator broke into the silence to ask if they had finished.

'No,' Blair said angrily, 'We haven't started yet.'

'Sorry,' she said, 'but there's a bloke trying to get through from Melbourne with the greasy wool prices.'

'Sod the greasy wool prices!' he shouted down the instrument. 'Clear the line.'

Burton, at his end, was enjoying Blair's embarrassment, even though he had been woken up at three in the morning to take the call.

'However,' he added generously, 'we can talk about that some other time.'

'How high can I go for those engines?' Blair asked, his voice flat.

'Get the chap down to a hundred thousand,' Burton said, 'and I'll send you a draft tomorrow.'

'Dollars or pounds?' Blair queried.

'Dollars, of course. Good-bye. Give my love to Monica.' He put the phone down and smiled.

'Was it *so* amusing?' asked the red-head from the next pillow.

'Hilarious,' said Burton. 'I have to find fifty thousand pounds to keep my wife away with her lover for a couple more days.'

'I hope you think it's worth it,' she purred, snuggling up to him.

'Whether it is or not,' Burton said, 'I haven't the slightest idea where I'm going to look for it.'

By the morning he had it all worked out. But he would need an ally. He packed his personal assistant off to his office and rang Red-Air.

'Burton here,' he said. 'I want to speak to Paul Blair.'

When Blair told Monica that Burton had decided to force their affair out into the open, she just laughed.

'He was just trying to throw you off balance over the money,' she said. 'He's known about it ever since it first started. He doesn't give a damn.'

'Then why choose this particular moment?' Blair asked. 'I mean apart from playing games over the money?'

'I don't know,' she said. 'Charles likes to choose his time, and it's always part of a set of moves worked out in advance.' She thought for a moment, then took his hand. 'He may have decided that one of us is dispensable, darling. But at the moment, I'm not sure which of us.'

'Do you think we should get straight back and find out what's going on?' Blair asked.

'I thought you were shopping for engines?'

'I doubt if I can even buy one engine with that money,' Blair said.

She withdrew her hand.

'If that's the only consideration at the moment,' she said with a touch of coolness, 'then you'd better book the flights straight back home.'

'It's the reason I came,' he said. 'But over the past couple of days I've found a very good reason to stay. I think I could be very happy in this wilderness with you for a long, long time.'

She relaxed again and kissed him on the cheek.

'Let's just make it a couple more days,' she said. 'As for the auction, well, you might just be lucky.'

It was the word 'auction' that suddenly struck a chord in Blair's mind. The following day his own cottage was up for auction; he'd completely forgotten about it. Not that it really demanded his presence, and in any case Paul would probably remember it.

But Paul Blair had other things on his mind. First of all there was Kim. He had been in love a couple of times in his short life, so he knew all the symptoms, or thought he did. You lay awake at night going over every scrap of conversation you had had with the girl during the day, searching each word or phrase for subtle meanings, hints that your feelings were reciprocated. You woke early in the morning with a tremendous sense of excitement at meeting her again, tinged with the fear that on this particular day you would say something wrong, or she would take something the wrong way and it would all be over. But the real test was the time when you were away from her. If an hour seemed like a week and a whole weekend like eternity you were definitely in love and there wasn't a damn thing you could do about it. The Saturday afternoon shopping trip, the bane of every married man's life, was as exciting as a trip to a South Sea island to Paul. Tea at the flat had been as delightful as it was unexpected. He had not really expected her to agree. Learning about her past was like exploring a new world, but the best thing of all that happened on that memorable Saturday was her promise to come out with him the following day.

Later in the evening when she had rung to call it off on

the grounds that she had to go into the office at Burton's instruction, he felt totally dejected. He immediately offered to go in and work with her, but she said there wasn't much point as he would have nothing to do and she wanted to concentrate. He was convinced it must be an excuse. She had thought about it and decided she did not want to see him. One thing was perfectly clear, she thought more of Burton than she did of him or she would not have run to do his bidding. He had been wondering about her relationship with Burton for some time. She always seemed to defer to him, and the looks they exchanged from time to time seemed to Paul's heightened perception to convey rather more than a business relationship. Burton must be at least fifteen years older than her, of course, but women often fancied older men. As he lay in bed that night he resolved he would have it out with Kim. He must know. He would find an excuse to ask her directly – in a roundabout way.

But when Monday came he found he hadn't the courage. It would have to be done away from the office, if he could ever find an excuse to see her alone again. Perhaps another shopping trip.

Then, out of the blue, came the call from Burton himself. Paul was convinced it must have something to do with what he now regarded as his frustrated romance with Kim. Perhaps Burton wanted a man-to-man talk. She had obviously told him about it all. Very well, he was ready for it. The only thing that puzzled Paul was that Burton had seemed quite friendly on the phone and asked him to come up to London and bring all the company's account books and ledgers. But then knowing Burton, this was no doubt a ruse. He would get him up there on the pretext of discussing business, maybe even do so, then, later on warn him to keep away from Kim or else.

On the train up to London, Paul worked out the response he would make. It would be something on the lines of '. . . well, Mr Burton, it's either me or you and may the best man win'. He might have to find a more novel phrasing, but something along those lines.

It was the penthouse itself that daunted his spirit. He had never seen anything quite so luxurious except in films. A persistent voice in the back of his mind warned him of the laws of the jungle – never fight on your opponent's territory: it gave him a psychological advantage. He looked around at the Chinese silk rugs, buffalo hide upholstery and Italian light fittings and knew he'd lost on that score before he even started.

Burton seemed affable and relaxed. He offered Paul coffee the moment he arrived and suggested they would have a working buffet lunch later on, was smoked salmon all right? Paul knew that you should never accept a rival's hospitality either, as it lowered your guard, but he hadn't had smoked salmon for donkey's years and found himself agreeing.

They settled down to examine Red-Air's accounts. Burton implied that it was simply a routine check, but he didn't miss a thing. Luckily, Paul could justify every item of expenditure and kept everything up to date. By the end of the morning session, Burton congratulated him on the way Paul had presented the figures and come to grips with the complexity of the business so rapidly. The only query he had was on Paul's own salary.

'It seems to me a little on the low side for the job you're doing, Paul,' he said.

'My father said we couldn't afford any more at the moment,' Paul said guardedly, 'and I'm quite happy with it.'

'I'll have a word with your father about that,' Burton said. 'I think we can do a little better than that for you now the business is under way.'

A Filipino in a white coat materialized from nowhere with the smoked salmon, a delicious side salad and a bottle of Chablis.

Paul thought he should decline the Chablis as he wanted

to keep a clear head. He knew that all this charm and praise and the offer of a rise must be the smile on the face of the serpent before striking at the jugular, but found himself drinking it just the same. Half an hour later he was beginning to feel quite light-headed and decided that he must have misjudged this man after all. Burton hadn't mentioned Kim at all. Burton started talking about the books again.

'Paul,' he said genially, 'if you were an independent auditor looking at these accounts from the outside, how would you assess the profitability of Red-Air?'

'I'd say it was just about keeping its head above water,' Paul said.

'Supposing you'd been asked to recommend the company to a finance house for a short-term loan of, say, fifty thousand pounds. Could you feel justified in doing that?'

Paul had to think hard about that.

'I think I should want to know if there was any collateral apart from the fixed assets,' he said.

'Exactly,' said Burton. 'Now you see, Paul, we have a problem. I had a call during the night from your father for that amount. He needs it urgently to buy spare parts. Neither of us would want to let him down, so have you any thoughts on how I could raise it by, say, four o'clock this afternoon?'

'I think we'd have to do it on the basis of advance orders,' Paul said.

'But on paper, those orders scarcely match the projected expenditure, so I don't think that's going to impress anyone, do you?' Burton said.

Paul admitted that this was true.

'I think we have to produce something more convincing than that,' Burton went on. 'Supposing there was another quarter of a million in the pipeline due to be paid into the company's account over the next few days?'

'I'd want proof of that,' Paul said. 'Signed contracts.'

'Of course,' Burton said. He crossed to his bureau desk and returned a moment later with a large brown envelope.

'I am going to show you something in complete confidence, Paul,' Burton said. 'But for the time being, I must ask you not to reveal the contents to anyone, even your father. Is that understood?'

'Providing there's nothing in it that could harm my father,' Paul said loyally.

'Quite the contrary. It gives evidence of the back-up finance that both this company and your father need if we are all to stay afloat,' he said.

He shook out the contents of the envelope. There were two copies of a contract, one in French, the other in English. Burton waited while Paul scanned through the English version. It was an agreement to supply agricultural machinery from a supplier in Belgium to a Greek company, but delivery was to be made in the Sudan. It was signed with a Greek name he couldn't read on the one part and Burton on the other on behalf of one of his companies registered in Lausanne. The contract was worth two million pounds sterling. Twenty-five per cent of that figure was to be paid in advance.

Paul looked puzzled.

'I don't understand,' he said. 'What's this got to do with Red-Air?'

'Red-Air will be flying it out there,' Burton said. 'I'm allowing for half the advance figure mentioned to cover the cost of transport. That's the quarter of a million I said was in the pipeline.'

'Is there a separate contract to cover that?' Paul asked.

'That's being prepared in my office at this moment, between my Lausanne company and Red-Air as carriers,' Burton said.

'Then why is it all so secret that I mustn't tell anyone?' Paul asked. 'Everyone in the office will know when you lodge the carrier's contract with us.'

'Of course,' Burton said. 'But I don't wish to do that

quite yet. You see, there may be some objections on the Red-Air board.'

He meant from Monica, but he didn't name her.

'I don't see anything wrong with carrying agricultural machinery to the Sudan,' Paul said.

'Let us just say that the term "agricultural machinery" is a euphemism,' Burton said carefully.

'You mean it's really another arms contract.'

'So I'm led to believe,' Burton said. 'Belgium tends to specialize in the manufacture of small arms. But I really don't want to raise that hare at the moment, the first job is to include that quarter of a million as an item of income in your accounts. This will give us a healthy cash balance and convince my bankers we are safe for a fifty-thousand-pound loan. Do you understand?'

'No,' said Paul. 'If there's a quarter of a million coming in, we don't need the loan.'

'Your father needs the money *now*,' Burton said patiently. 'Over the next twenty-four hours. That means I have to raise it this afternoon.'

Paul began to sober up rapidly. He was beginning to get the picture.

'Are you suggesting I show a quarter of a million in the accounts before it's actually arrived, Mr Burton?' he asked.

'Why not?' Burton asked. 'It'll be here in a few days and it's covered by contracts.'

'Then why not just show those contracts to your bankers?' Paul said.

'My Greek partners don't want them to know about their involvement in the deal,' Burton said vaguely. 'I don't know why, but doubtless they have their own reasons.'

Paul knew it was a lie. If Burton's bankers wouldn't advance against the Greek contract it must mean that they didn't regard the contract as safe. Either that, or it was some kind of complicated tax fiddle and the money wouldn't pass through the bank at all.

'How do we know the Greeks are going to pay up?' he asked.

'They'll pay the advance on this contract the moment we have completed the present shipment to Abu Dhabi,' Burton said. 'That's why I've been rushing that one through over the past few days. But the chap I deal with is absolutely straight and I can personally guarantee the money will be through by the end of the week. In fact, I'm going to Athens tomorrow to collect it.'

Paul felt a cold sweat breaking out on his face. Burton was asking him to falsify Red-Air's accounts to show a substantial item of income as having been paid in when there was nothing but Burton's word to say they'd ever receive it.

'I'm a certified accountant, Mr Burton,' he said. 'I could be struck off for making a false entry in the ledgers. In any case, it couldn't be supported by our own bank statements.'

'As a certified accountant, I'm sure my people will take your word for it, but if there's any problems I'll tell them you'll send them a bank statement later on. By that time the money will have arrived,' Burton said. He leaned forward and put his hand on Paul's thigh reassuringly. 'I have to do it this way to help your father buy that spare engine, Paul,' he said. 'It's for his benefit, not for mine. And there's really nothing wrong in making up accounts ahead of time. One often has to do it for tax reasons.'

Burton felt Paul's thigh muscles tighten under his hand and wondered whether this was from his ethical dilemma or simply a sensual reaction. When Paul spoke again it was from a dry throat. His voice was hoarse.

'I'm sorry, Mr Burton, I can't do it and you have no right to ask me to,' he said.

Burton watched Paul's reactions with interest. The last statement could be taken either way. He relaxed his grip on the boy's thigh until it was no more than a gentle touch. His mind wandered for a fleeting moment to memories of chubby newspaper boys. Then he smiled into Paul's face. It was a feminine, seductive smile.

'Paul,' he said quietly, 'I promised your mother I would keep an eye on your career. But I needed to know first that I could trust you as an honest accountant. You have just proved that I can. I can't tell you how delighted I am.'

He gave the boy a final pat, rose quickly and crossed to his bureau desk. Paul felt a wave of relief pass through his whole body. So Burton had just been putting him to the test. Thank God he had stuck to his guns. He was now totally confused about this strange man. Everyone had taken it for granted he was a slick operator entirely without scruples. But perhaps it was just an act he kept up to impress people. Charles Burton may yet turn out to be a sheep in wolf's clothing, Paul thought. Suddenly this explained Kim's reaction to him. Maybe Kim knew this all along. This would explain a lot. He felt the time had come to raise the subject.

'Mr Burton, how long have you known Kim Hayward?' he asked tentatively.

Burton had his back to him, seated at the bureau. He didn't turn round. 'Some years,' he said. 'At least, I knew her father rather better. His firm once built a factory for me. Did me a great favour. We were desperate to get it finished on time, he and his chaps worked all over one Christmas for me. I used them as much as I could after that.'

'He went bankrupt, I heard,' Paul said.

'Yes, very sad. Too good a craftsman, that was the trouble. Couldn't compete with the jerrybuilders. Luckily I was in a position to help him over the worst of it, but then he had a heart attack.'

'And did you go on helping him?' Paul asked.

Burton shrugged. 'A little.'

He turned round to face Paul, as though slightly embarrassed at being found out doing a kind action.

'I was wondering why Kim seems to think so much of you,' Paul said.

'Does she?' Burton asked. 'I really had no idea. She's a funny girl. Bit of a father complex. She had a crush on Mason for a while.' He smiled. 'It put her in a bit of a spot when I suddenly turned up again out of the blue to buy his company. But she's sorted herself out now.'

Then abruptly he changed the subject. He got up from the bureau, glanced at his watch and said, 'Well, if I'm going to make my appointment at the bank, you'd better get a move on and update those ledgers to include the quarter of a million. Then I can take the accounts with me.'

Paul gaped at Burton in astonishment.

'What's the matter now, Paul?'

'I just said I wouldn't do it,' Paul stuttered.

Then he saw that Burton had a cheque in his hand. He had been writing it out at the bureau desk.

'Get it into Red-Air's account within the next hour,' he said. 'That should do the trick.'

Paul took it with unsteady fingers and glanced at it. It was made out for a quarter of a million pounds on a Lausanne bank.

'You're paying the money over before it arrives?' Paul said, stupefied.

'I told you I have complete confidence in my Greek partners,' Burton said.

He knew it would take four or five days to clear, and that was a lifetime at the speed Burton moved. All he had to do now was get the money out of Nick Varos before the Lausanne cheque bounced.

And raise the fifty thousand from his merchant bank, of course. It didn't prove as easy as he hoped, he was already heavily overdrawn on their account, but they finally agreed when he was able to show them evidence of a very profitable-looking air cargo company he happened to part own on the side. They only made one condition before parting with the money, that he should lodge his shareholding in

Red-Air with them as collateral. But he even slipped out of that one by lodging Monica's shares instead. His silly red-headed personal assistant had made a mistake when they were drawn up and put them in Burton's own name. Monica had never bothered to ask to look at them.

That evening he flew to Athens to coincide with the arrival of Red-Air's Britannia carrying the final arms shipment to Abu Dhabi.

Survival in business, Charles Burton always maintained, was largely a question of timing.

The auction for spare parts from Morphett's crashed Britannia was an informal affair. Two Malayan Chinese, a cargo operator from Darwin and a representative from an aviation spares agency were bidding against Blair for the engines. Morphett had commandeered a couple of tables in the airport bar for the job. It meant no one had to go far to get beer.

The first engine went to the Chinese for $120,000. After that, Blair didn't think there was a lot of point in staying, it was over the limit that Burton had allowed him, even for one engine, and he had now given up any chance of taking two away. But the Chinese had obviously only intended to buy one as they dropped out of the bidding for the second. The agency man pulled out at $95,000, which left only Blair and the Darwin man. It was he who had pushed the Chinese up on the first engine before dropping out at $118,000. He did the same again to Blair. When they topped the hundred grand mark, Blair kept his hands firmly on the table. Morphett looked at him and grinned.

'Come on, Tony,' he said. 'You didn't come all this way to go back empty-handed.'

'Sorry mate,' said Blair. 'You're over my limit.'

'It's still dirt cheap,' Morphett said. 'You'll regret it.'

'That's my tough luck,' Blair said. He finished his drink and left.

He went back to the hotel to collect Monica and told her that her husband's stinginess had cost them a good cheap engine they desperately needed.

'Never mind,' she said. 'It's been a wonderful trip.' She kissed him. They got their bags together and called a cab to take them back to the airport to start the long journey back.

As they reached the airport bar for a final drink before leaving Oodnadatta, they found Morphett and the Darwin man leaning up against the bar. Morphett hailed them cheerfully.

'Come and have a drink on us, Tony,' he said. 'I'd like you to meet my mate, Rod. Rod, this is Tony, and this is Monica; Monica, this is Rod.'

'We've already met,' said Blair, trying not to sound sour. He shook hands with Rod nevertheless and asked him where he operated from.

'I'm on the meat run,' Rod said. 'Darwin to the Middle East.'

This was a favourite run for long-haul operators, taking Australian beef for the rich sheiks' tables.

'In a Britannia?' Blair asked in surprise. 'That's a bit of a haul, isn't it?'

Rod laughed. 'You've got to be joking, Tony. I fly 707s. I wouldn't have a turbo-prop as a gift.'

'Then what did you want that engine for?' Blair asked.

'Just doing my old mate a favour by pushing the bids up for the Chinks,' he said. 'It's no bloody good to me.'

'You mean the auction was rigged,' said Monica indignantly.

Both men laughed. Morphett turned to Blair.

'You can have it for a hundred grand,' Morphett said. 'Seeing as you're a decent bloke.'

'It would serve you bloody right if I left you stuck with it,' Blair said.

'I'll tell you what I'll do for you,' said Morphett. 'I'll get my mate to take it up to Darwin on a cattle truck, then

Rod can put it on a 707 and run it to Saudi for you. Can you pick it up from Saudi?'

'No problem,' said Blair.

He bought them both a drink, fixed a price with Rod for the freight charge and it was done.

That was the great thing about Australia, Blair said to Monica afterwards. Everyone had a mate who somehow or other came in useful.

'Do you really think he came all the way down from Darwin just to push up the bidding for his friend?' Monica asked.

Blair laughed.

'That was just a bonus. He came because he smelt cargo. He's probably done a deal with the Chinese to fly their engine back as well.'

They left Pete to handle the shipment and flew back for the promised night in Sydney. In the morning they went up to the surfing beach at Dee Why and swam in the giant Pacific breakers. That afternoon, reluctantly, they boarded the flight back to London. Neither knew what they were going to find when they got back. But at that moment they didn't care.

In the small conference room at the Eagle, Stanwick, another auction was taking place. Paul Blair, elated by his budding romance with Kim and still in a state of indecision over Charles Burton's activities, only remembered it at the last minute.

By the time he arrived, the auctioneer's hammer was going down for the last time at £62,000 for his father's cottage.

'Sold,' said the auctioneer, 'to the lady at the back.'

He looked in astonishment as the lady at the back reached for her cheque book. It was his mother.

8

Captain Robertson was worried. The Red-Air Britannia seemed to be using a heck of a lot more oil than she should on the return leg from the Middle East. She had been topped up at Abu Dhabi, but the pressure was down again when they stopped at Nicosia for fuel. While Robertson supervised the loading – they were picking up a payload of Cyprus grapes for the return leg – his flight engineer checked for possible leaks. But they could find no obvious cause, so topped up again and hoped for the best. Robertson knew the aircraft had had this trouble before. It was an oil pressure drop that had caused the engine change at the last CAA check, but the problem had not gone away entirely. The old lady seemed to be having a drinking problem.

Robertson sympathized with her, but she was getting other ailments at the same time. On the voyage before this he had trouble getting her nosewheel down on landing and had to blow it down with an oxygen bottle. Maybe she was getting rheumatism in the joints as well, he thought. He also noticed she was reacting a fraction late on a tight turn to port. They had carefully checked ailerons and rudder but couldn't find the cause. He knew that no aircraft of this age was without fault, but when the faults started to come thick and fast it was time she had a few days' rest. She had been flying for three days solid, so it wasn't really surprising. He had reported each fault to Mason as it occurred, but the company seemed intent on flying the aircraft till it dropped of exhaustion. Tony Blair,

Robertson felt sure, would have refused to allow the last flight, but Blair wasn't back from Aussie yet. As they started out on the final leg of the voyage, he hoped and prayed they would make it back to Stanwick in one piece.

Half an hour after they reached their ceiling height over the Aegean, the fire warning sounded. It was number one engine. He closed it down immediately and there were some tense moments on the flight deck as he and his engineer strained their eyes out of the windows for the telltale signs of smoke. But there was nothing. Gingerly he opened the engine up again. The warning hooter stopped as suddenly as it began. They all breathed again.

'Spurious fire warning,' said his first officer in relief.

'I wouldn't bet on it,' Robertson said. Small fires sometimes went out of their own accord, but never without leaving some damage behind.

'If we're going to get this old lady back home,' he said, 'we're going to need a hell of a lot of luck.'

Somewhere far below them, another man's luck had just run out.

When Burton landed at Athens airport, he made straight for Omonia Square in the city centre. He decided not to warn Nick Varos he was coming. Varos had a habit of laying on an evening's wild entertainment in the Plaka when business contacts came to call, with a lot of girls and a lot more ouzo. Burton didn't feel like a boozy night out. He just wanted to collect his money and head straight back to London. Greek hospitality tended to go on all night.

When he got to the office it was locked and no one answered his insistent knock. He went to the nearest phone booth and rang the office number, but there was no reply. He searched his mind to try and remember if it was a public holiday or saint day. The Greeks seemed to have so many of them. But the bustle of activity in the square outside seemed to indicate a normal trading day.

He searched his address book for the number of Varos's private apartment. When the apartment phone rang for five minutes without an answer he began to get seriously worried. It was not like Varos to leave a telephone unattended, his business depended on unexpected calls from some distant part of the world at some unlikely hour.

He spent the rest of the afternoon hunting down the few business colleagues of Varos that he knew of. But none of them had heard from him for several days. He had last been heard of in the Middle East, but, as several of the businessmen pointed out, Varos travelled widely, from Washington to Moscow, and was by nature so secretive that no one could be certain where he was to be found at any time. The general opinion seemed to be that the arms dealer was either abroad or had gone to ground, but no one could explain why his office was closed and his staff had apparently disappeared without trace.

It was early evening before Burton remembered that once, in a night club at Sounion, he had met Varos's brother. It had only been a brief meeting, and the only thing Burton could recall was that the brother's name was Christos and that he was in shipping. Since nearly every wealthy Greek Burton had ever met seemed to have something to do with shipping, this wasn't much of a clue, but at least it was something. He felt he now needed a base to work from, so he checked into the Hilton and started ringing around the main shipping lines. By the time he had tracked down a Christos Varos it was late and the shipping office was closed except for a night watchman. He spoke only Greek and Burton had to get the Hilton telephone operator to translate for him.

Christos Varos, the nightwatchman said, had gone home to his village that morning to attend his brother's funeral.

Janet Blair moved into the cottage on the day following the auction. The estate agent warned her that she would be trespassing until the legal conveyancing was complete, but she paid the full amount on the spot and demanded the key. All that legal nonsense, she said, could be sorted out later. She now had her old home back.

'But why?' Paul had asked the previous evening when she took him to dinner. 'I mean, are you really going to live there, Mother?'

'You surely don't think I paid all that money just to keep it as a memento, Paul,' she said.

'But . . . isn't it rather large for one person?' he asked.

Janet smiled.

'Your father lived there alone for ten years. At least, nominally so. I've no doubt he had overnight guests,' she added. 'Perhaps I shall do the same.'

'You can't be serious,' he said.

She looked at her son with amusement.

'Why not, Paul? What's sauce for the gander is sauce for the goose. If your father could use it to entertain his air hostesses, why shouldn't I have it for my lovers?'

'But why *that* particular house?' Paul said. 'I mean you could do that anywhere.'

'I happen to like that cottage,' she said. 'I always did. There's a part of me still there.'

Paul laughed nervously.

'Dad will get the surprise of his life when he gets back.'

'Yes,' she said. 'Won't he just.'

'But if you really wanted the place,' Paul said, 'why didn't you just deal with Dad direct and save the cost of the auction?'

'The cost is on the vendor, dear,' she smiled. 'Not on the buyer.'

'Then that's not really fair on him, is it?' Paul said.

'I didn't make the decision to put the place up for

auction. He did. Before I arrived,' she said. 'So that cost would have been incurred anyway.'

She ordered champagne to celebrate. But she hardly touched her own, leaving Paul to get steadily drunk.

Then she said, 'Paul, are you quite happy in that rather nasty bachelor flat?'

'Yes,' he said. 'So long as my father shares it with me.'

'Has it occurred to you that you might be rather cramping his style?'

'What do you mean, Mother?' he said.

'You must know he's having an affair with Monica Burton.'

'Yes,' he admitted. 'At least, I suppose that's what it is.'

Janet smiled patronizingly.

'You *suppose*! You surely don't think she went off to Australia with him just to carry his suitcases.'

'No,' he admitted. He was starting to feel uncomfortable. He hated being caught in the crossfire when his mother was making her traditionally acid remarks about his father. But she carried on relentlessly.

'Don't you think it's a bit hard on them that they have to go halfway round the world in order to sleep together because her husband's in her place and you're in his, Paul?' she said.

It was one of his mother's typical exaggerations, but it held enough truth to make Paul realize he might possibly be playing gooseberry.

'That's a ridiculous idea, Mother,' he said. 'They could get a hotel somewhere if they just wanted to . . .' He trailed off. She often wondered how she could possibly have reared such a prudish child.

'But that's so sordid, Paul,' Janet said reprovingly. 'In any case, supposing they felt like a more permanent relationship. What would you do then, stay on as an embarrassed lodger?'

Paul looked at her wide-eyed.

'You really think she'd leave Charles Burton for my father?' he asked.

'Well, that's not very complimentary to your dear old dad,' she laughed.

'I meant, the luxury life, the penthouse . . . all that,' he stuttered.

'Oh, Paul,' she said, 'be your age. She's the type of woman who gets a kick out of pigging it for a bit. I don't suppose it would last, but they might give it a try for six months.'

'In that case, I would obviously move out,' he said.

She moved in for the *coup de grâce.*

'Then why not do it now, Paul? Before they get back.'

'Take a flat of my own, you mean.'

'No, darling,' Janet said gently. 'Come home. Did you really think I paid all that money to buy the old house just to take lovers? It's our home, Paul. You love it as well as I do.'

He flushed red with anger.

'Then why did you ever leave it?' he said. 'Why did you take me away from it as a child! Why didn't you two stay together, for God's sake!'

She saw that there were tears in his eyes. She reached out and took his hand. 'Paul, darling,' she said. 'These things happen. At the time it seemed impossible to keep the marriage together. And I was in love with Alan. Later on I knew it couldn't last, but everyone is entitled to search for happiness even if they don't always find it. But that period of our lives is all over now. Fate moves in circles . . .'

'Oh, for God's sake, Mother, don't start on all that rubbish about fate again.' He suddenly realized there were people coming into the restaurant and tried to keep his voice down. 'It wasn't fate that brought *me* here. I wanted to see Dad again. Now I know why you only put up a token resistance back in Salisbury, because you wanted me to do just that! Then you had an excuse to follow me. That wasn't blind fate, it was contrivance on *your* part.'

'Well,' she said thoughtfully, 'sometimes you have to give fate a little push. But it all comes to the same thing in the end. All three of us are back again in the one place. Wouldn't it be nice to be a family again?'

There was a moment's pause as Paul grasped the real meaning of what his mother was saying.

'You mean . . . you want to marry Dad again?' he said at last.

'I don't know,' Janet said slowly. 'But it would be a fascinating experiment, wouldn't it. To see if we have really become more compatible by being apart.'

'He'd never agree to that!' Paul said vehemently. 'I know he wouldn't.'

She smiled again.

'I doubt if you know your father *quite* as well as I do, Paul,' she said.

'But what about Monica?' Paul said. 'A little while back you were saying . . .'

'That they might try it for six months.' She completed the sentence for him. 'On the other hand it may only be a matter of weeks if Charles Burton puts his foot down. In the meantime, the least we can do is provide your father with a home to come back to when it's over. Shall we do that, darling?'

When Blair and Monica landed at Heathrow, they both went their separate ways, he to Stanwick, she back to the penthouse. She arrived to find it empty. A message on the recording machine told her Charles had gone suddenly to Athens and would be back that night. She decided to wait up for him. There was a lot to discuss about their future. But by two in the morning when he still wasn't back, she decided to go to bed. Their discussion would now have to wait until the morning.

He must have got in sometime during the early hours,

but he didn't go to bed. When she got up and went into the kitchen she found him sitting at the table over coffee. He was looking drawn and haggard.

'Good trip?' he asked listlessly.

'Fine,' she said. 'And yours?'

'We have a problem,' Burton said.

'We have a number,' she replied. 'Do you feel like sorting them out now?'

'Perhaps we ought to take them one at a time,' he said.

Monica had never seen him looking quite so dejected.

'All right then, Charles, let's start with yours.'

He waited for her to pour herself some coffee, then said carefully, 'A man who owes me an awful lot of money has been careless enough to get himself shot.'

'Your Greek friend?'

'Yes,' he said.

'Who shot him?'

Burton shrugged. 'I haven't the slightest idea. He had so many enemies.'

'Well,' Monica said lightly, 'I've no doubt he deserved it. If a man lives by selling death to others, it's only natural justice he should have a taste of his own medicine.'

'You don't seem to understand,' Burton said. 'Varos died owing me half the money on that last shipment and . . . well, quite a lot of money for something else. It's money I've already committed.'

'Can't you claim from his company, or his estate, or something?' Monica asked.

'He kept his money in tax havens,' Burton said miserably. 'I doubt if his widow even knows where to look for it. As for his various companies, they've melted away like snow.'

'It's not like you to keep all your eggs in one basket, Charles,' Monica said.

'No,' he said painfully. 'I was gambling and I lost. The trouble is, they weren't even my eggs.'

He told her of the cheque for a quarter of a million

he had made out to Red-Air and could now not be met, of other cheques he had made out over the past few days in order to juggle money in and out of his various enterprises, all of which hinged on the Varos deals. She had never known him to be so frank about his activities. She ought to have felt some sympathy for him, but found she didn't.

'Well,' she said cheerfully, 'you've always managed to pick yourself up off the floor in the past, Charles. I'm sure you'll find a way of doing it again.'

'I'm touched by your faith in my abilities, Monica,' Burton said thinly. 'But this time I'm down to rock bottom. I shall have to cash every asset we own.'

'Such as?'

'This apartment, the cars, the pictures, even the rugs. How would you feel about that, darling?'

'You don't have to ask me, Charles. They're not mine and never have been. They're yours and you can do as you want with them.'

He looked at her steadily.

'You're prepared to give all this up, Monica?' he asked.

This was the moment when she should have told him she was prepared to give him up as well, but she couldn't find the words for it. It would look as though she was abandoning him because he was now penniless. Now that would have to wait for a more propitious moment.

'I really don't care that much about those things,' was all she could muster. 'I have my own income. No one's going to starve. And there's still Red-Air.'

'No, darling,' he said. 'That will have to be sold as well, I'm afraid.'

She stiffened.

'You can sell your shares in it, if you can find a buyer,' she said coldly. 'I've no intention of selling mine.'

'Yours are already at the pawnshop,' he said quietly.

The phone rang before she could recover from her shock.

It was Blair, calling from Stanwick. He sounded angry.

'Burton,' he growled over the phone, 'I want a board meeting.'

'Yes,' said Burton. 'So do I.'

'Then get your arse down here right away,' he said and slammed the phone down.

The Britannia sat on the parking lot looking like a patient on the operating table. Two engine cowlings were already stripped off. Engineers and fitters were swarming all over it. Cables from the ground-power unit were being fed into it like blood plasma tubes. The old lady was very sick.

Blair and Mason were dodging around peering into vital parts of her anatomy when Kim came running across from the Portakabins to say that the Burtons had arrived.

Without a word, both men strode back towards the offices to start the board meeting.

Blair wasted no time with the niceties of an agenda and the reading of minutes. He turned on Burton the moment he came through the door. 'What the hell have you been doing while I was away?' he shouted. 'You risked the lives of my crew flying that aircraft to death. It was only because Robertson's a damn fine pilot that he got her back at all!'

Burton looked at him in surprise.

'You know perfectly well I know nothing about the technical side, Blair,' he said. 'I left that to Captain Mason.'

Mason stared down at the desk, chewing his lip.

'I've already torn him off a strip,' Blair said. 'He maintains you were calling the shots.'

'The aircraft had to earn money,' Burton said. 'I thought we'd all agreed that.'

'Not at the risk of human lives,' Blair said angrily.

Mason looked up sheepishly. 'We checked her over pretty thoroughly before the last voyage, Tony,' he said.

'Bullshit,' said Blair. 'You couldn't have had the time. You let yourself be conned into it.'

'What exactly is the damage to the plane?' Monica asked.

'We don't know yet,' Blair said. 'I've ordered a thorough overhaul, and I'm calling in specialist engineers from the manufacturers.'

'What's all that going to cost us?' Burton asked. Monica's intervention had given him a moment to recover from Blair's attack.

'I've no idea,' Blair snapped. 'But she doesn't move from that parking lot until I know she's fit to fly. I'm not even sure she ever will be.'

It was the answer Burton wanted.

'Then perhaps we ought to put the aircraft up for sale right now,' he said. 'And wind up the company.'

'Now wait a minute,' Mason said in alarm. 'There's no need to go to those lengths. That Brit's had things go wrong with her before, we've always got them right. Let's wait on a bit till we get the engineer's report.'

'I don't think Charles can afford to wait,' Monica said. She turned to Blair. 'He wants to sell to raise cash and you've just given him the perfect excuse.'

'Let's not jump the gun,' Burton said hastily. He was furious with her for showing all his cards, but there was nothing he could do.

For the next five minutes she held the floor, telling the whole board exactly what she now knew. That they were never going to get the last payment for the arms shipment so all the hassle had been for nothing, that her husband was now in desperate trouble.

'He even paid a dud cheque for a quarter of a million into this company's funds,' she added. 'I should like to move a motion that he resigns from the board of Red-Air forthwith.'

Burton was down to his last card.

'If that is the feeling of the meeting,' he said calmly, 'then I am perfectly willing to do so. But I should warn you that your problems won't end.' He looked bleakly at Monica. 'My wife has accused me of fraudulently passing a cheque knowing there were no funds to meet it. That is a criminal offence, and doubtless if you wished to pursue it through the courts I could go to jail.' He paused for effect, then looked directly at Blair. 'But I might not be the only one to pay the penalty,' he said. 'Your own son entered that amount into the company's accounts and conspired with me to raise a loan on the basis of it. Whether he pleads ignorance or not, if there was a fraud, he was party to it.'

He rose from the table in the stunned silence that followed.

'I've no doubt you'll wish to discuss the implications of all this without my presence,' he said thinly, then collected his briefcase and walked out.

The meeting went on for the next three hours while they tried to pick up the pieces from the havoc that Charles Burton had left behind. When it finally ended they all knew they had resolved nothing. The only thing anyone could do was to wait to see if the Britannia would ever fly again. For without that aircraft there wasn't even the tattered shreds of a company.

But the game old lady on the parking lot was not yet ready to give up the ghost. Since retiring in middle age from service with the RAF, she had undergone more tissue and organ transplants than a Miami matriarch. And she clung on to life just as stubbornly.

When the engineer's report finally landed on Blair's desk, he studied it with a growing feeling of optimism. The number one engine had not caught fire. The warning must have been spurious and was probably caused by overheating when the oil pressure dropped. The cause of the troublesome oil drop could not be ascertained with certainty, but they had changed a couple of seals that looked as though they might have been at the bottom of the trouble. The fault with the nosewheel mechanism had been traced to hydraulic failure with a simultaneous hiccup in the back-up systems. The engineers thought it might have been due to impregnation with fine sand from the desert, but the mechanism now seemed to be working perfectly.

The cause of the late reactions to rudder controls could not be traced, and Blair called Captain Robertson in to discuss it with him again.

'You must have been pretty tired on that voyage, Lee. And worried,' Blair said. 'You're sure you didn't imagine it?'

'Could be,' Robertson admitted. 'Sometimes, when you're flaked out, it's your own reactions that are a fraction slow and you blame it on the aircraft.'

That seemed fair enough. At all events, Blair felt, it was not a crucial fault so long as every pilot was aware it could happen.

He discussed the situation with Mason. Neither of them mourned the loss of the arms shipments, and in fact their forward order book was actually looking quite healthy. Without Burton on their backs to bug them, they felt they might just stagger on. And Burton had suddenly gone very silent. Monica told Blair he had flown immediately to New York after the board meeting. She had no idea why as there was nothing but a cryptic message on the telephone recording machine. She said that her husband would doubtless turn up again soon with a brand-new scheme for self rescue, but for the moment she didn't seem too bothered.

They now had a message through from Riyadh that the Australian engine had arrived there and was waiting onward shipment to the UK.

'What do we do?' Mason asked. 'Have another carrier bring it over, or go and collect it ourselves?'

'It's cheaper if we do it,' Blair said. 'But I'm not prepared to risk a crew until that Brit's had a thorough air test.'

Mason thought for a moment.

'How about you and I taking the Riyadh trip,' he said. 'We can do the test on the way.'

It seemed a reasonable proposition. Both men knew the plane better than anyone. If there were still any faults, they were the best people to find them.

The Red-Air Britannia took off at dawn the following morning. They had a mixed payload on the outward leg: three tons of bathroom fittings for a new hotel in Malta, a drainage pump for Cairo that had been sent to the UK manufacturers for repair and was wanted back urgently, and some shopping for a sheik. The sheik seemed to have practically cleared Harrods china department in one fell swoop. He was obviously expecting a lot of people for dinner.

The plane took off like a bird, every one of the controls responding perfectly. It almost seemed as though the old lady was glad to get away from all those engineers and fitters shaking their heads solemnly over her.

Kim and Paul watched her leave from the office window. Paul felt that Kim seemed much more free and easy now that Burton had disappeared. She had promised him he could take her to dinner that evening, providing she paid her share. It proved a happy evening. They were joined by some young pilots and their girlfriends in the bar afterwards which took the edge off any serious conversation. Later she drove him back to his father's flat and they kissed good night. Sometime soon, he thought happily, he must buy a car of his own, then he could take her back to her own flat.

As he entered, he realized the light was on. He could not remember leaving it like that. In the centre of the room were two large packed suitcases. Seated in the armchair, trying hard to keep awake, was his mother. He could not think how she had got in, but she was like that. She would have made a marvellous cat burglar.

'Have a nice evening, darling?' she asked.

'What's all this, Mother?' he asked, looking at the suitcases.

'You promised you'd come to live with me,' Janet said. 'Your room's all ready.'

'I didn't promise,' Paul protested. 'You took it for granted.'

'I knew you wouldn't be able to tell your father,' she said. 'So I told him myself. It's all arranged.'

'He agreed?' Paul asked in astonishment.

'No,' she said. 'Not exactly. He said it was up to you to make your own decisions, but he certainly couldn't stop you.'

'That's right, Mother,' Paul said. 'It *is* up to me. And I'm staying here, so will you now please go.'

Janet looked at her son in speechless amazement. But before she had a chance to protest he had taken her by the arm and led her to the door. She left without a murmur.

Afterwards, Paul wondered how he had found the courage.

He also knew he wouldn't be able to keep it up. Janet was not baulked that easily.

Blair and Mason alternated in the left-hand seat, changing the pilot and co-pilot roles. This meant they could both have a go at feeling how the plane was flying and compare notes. She was flying beautifully. They dropped off their various payloads en route and stayed overnight at Riyadh. The next morning they supervised the loading of the spare engine and took off an hour after dawn. Mason was taking the first leg of the voyage in the pilot's seat. Blair would take over at Nicosia where they were due for a tech stop and to pick up another payload of grapes.

Out of Riyadh, they had a fairly steep bank to starboard. The aircraft responded five seconds late. Mason glanced across to Blair.

'Robertson was right,' he said. 'She's dragging.'

Once they reached their ceiling height, Mason tried

throwing the aircraft about a bit to see if it happened again. But it didn't.

'She's just being awkward,' Blair said. 'To make sure we don't take her for granted.'

But they were just that little bit more apprehensive from then on.

At Nicosia she landed and took off again perfectly.

'You know,' said Mason, 'I think I know what it's all about. She just doesn't like Arab airports. She used to play me up in Beirut.'

'Maybe she's Jewish,' Blair said.

Mason switched on the auto pilot and they broke for coffee.

Blair had a word with the flight engineer. It was his old mate, Pete, who had flown with him out of Ximbali.

'How's the oil pressure?'

'Keep your fingers crossed,' Pete said. Dour as ever. He stayed with his eyes glued to the gauges.

As the day wore on and no more faults showed up, Blair began to let his mind wander. It was nice to be back in the air away from it all. He thought of Monica and their glorious few days in South Australia. That was the way it should be. A few mad romantic days with a woman who didn't make too many demands on you, then back to the solitude of the air. But supposing Burton had left her for good. What then? Did he want Monica on a more permanent basis? She was beautiful, she was talented and amusing. He could do a hell of a lot worse. Well, wait and see. It's never a good idea to tempt fate by making plans.

It was the thought of fate that put Janet in his mind.

What was he going to do about her? When Paul told him she had bought the cottage he had burst out laughing. Poor Paul had just stood looking sheepish, as though he had expected his father to strike him down for being the bearer of bad news. But it really *was* funny. They had bought the place for £3000 all those years ago. Now she had forked out £62,000 to buy it back. Not her own money, of course. Alan's money. The man who had broken up their marriage. He wondered if the bugger would ever know how his settlement on Janet had been spent.

And all for what? A clumsy attempt to lure him back? 'No way,' Blair said, then he realized he had said it aloud.

'What did you say?' Mason asked.

'I was thinking of Janet,' Blair said.

Mason smiled. 'She's a clever woman,' he said.

'Yes,' said Blair. 'Too clever by half.'

But Mason went on smiling.

It was then that the hooter went.

'Fire,' shouted Pete. 'That bloody number one again.'

Blair shut it down immediately. They were still at ceiling height. Just coming over the English Channel. Stanwick was still an hour ahead.

As Robertson had done before, they waited and watched out of the window.

No smoke. Not even a trace.

'Spurious,' said Mason, breathing again.

'But what the hell's the cause of it?' Blair said. 'They were supposed to have checked all that!'

After a while he switched the motor back on. The warning remained silent.

'Slight pressure drop,' Pete said. But nothing serious. Yet.

They flew the last hour with eyes glued to the instruments.

They had just passed the outer Stanwick beacon when the warning sounded again. The same engine.

'Warn them I'm coming in on three,' Blair said to Mason.

'Ignore the bugger,' Mason said. 'It's a faulty warning.'

'I daren't risk it,' Blair said. And switched off his number one engine.

The next few minutes were spent in urgent exchanges with the tower as preparations were made on the airport for an emergency landing. They were now on the glide path and committed to land.

Blair had been warned over the radio that the weather was worsening, with fifty-mile-an-hour crosswinds over the airport, heavy, blinding rain and the cloudbase below 500 feet. But he was now on full flap and there was no chance of an overshoot even if he had the power available.

Suddenly, over the noise from the insistent fire hooter, Pete shouted, 'Christ, we're in trouble on two!'

Blair looked out of the window. Heavy black smoke was trailing out of the number two engine. The fire warning had fooled them; it was the second engine where the real trouble lay. No one had seen it from the ground because of the low cloud cover. He closed it down immediately. Now they were coming in on two motors, both on the same wing. He fought desperately with the rudder controls to keep her on line. But once again she was slow to respond. As she came in over the terminal buildings she began to shudder violently as though in her final death throe.

Paul and Kim stood transfixed on the taxiway, oblivious of the pelting rain. The fire engines were screaming past them towards the main runway. Two ambulances sped through the main gates and the barriers were closed behind them. There was nothing more anyone could do now but wait out the last few desperate moments. As the crippled aircraft lumbered towards them, fifty feet above the ground, Kim clung to Paul and closed her eyes. He could hear her starting to pray. But he could not avert his own eyes. It was his own father in that stricken aircraft, now, it seemed, only seconds away from certain death.

The Britannia hit the runway flatfooted, then bucked like a rearing horse. A moment before she settled for the second time, a crosswind caught her under the starboard wing. She slewed across the tarmac, then seemed to correct herself for a split second as Blair slammed the two good engines into reverse thrust. But it was not enough. On a dry runway her tyres would have given enough grip to steady her down, but half an inch of rain had turned the surface into a skidpan. With the brakes full on she started to aquaplane at seventy knots towards the grass verge, the outer engine still belching smoke, laced now with orange fingers of flame. The fire engines raced alongside her like sheepdogs, the snouts of their pressure hoses poised to douse her with foam. Behind them came the ambulances, hanging back at a respectful distance, waiting the signal to go in.

Inside the tiny cabin, the aircrew braced themselves for impact. All three men knew that the moment the aircraft stopped they would have only seconds to get clear. As the wheels ploughed into the soft earth, Blair felt the awful strain on the nosewheel as though it was an extension of his own limbs. The rain-sodden earth was like a sea of treacle, dragging the heavy aircraft by the head and throwing her weight forward. Then, with a crack like a rifle shot, the nosewheel snapped, her tail lifted and she dropped forward on her snout.

To Paul, the last moments seemed almost graceful. She appeared to have almost reached a stop when her head went down. Then the fire engines were surrounding her and in seconds she was white with foam. He started to run towards the stricken plane. He could see nothing now but the great arches of foam and the red carcasses of the fire trucks. Somewhere beneath the foam cascade he could see people moving about. He caught a glimpse of two firemen, one wielding an axe, the other carrying a ladder. An ambulance started to move close to the hull. He remembered thinking how brave all these people were to risk their lives to rescue the men inside when at any moment the aircraft could be enveloped in flame. Then, as he reached the perimeter of the accident area, he saw the Pax door open. Two men clambered out, then stooped and ran clear. It seemed an age before the third appeared. A tall figure, broad shouldered, poised in the doorway for a moment as though reluctant to leave. A moment later the figure turned snow white, dripping foam.

Then he heard his father bellowing like a bull.

'Take that bloody hose off me!'

Two firemen helped him down. He pushed them aside and started to run towards a waiting ambulance. But it was a strange, unfamiliar gait. His right leg seemed to be dragging in pain. Then, as Paul ran towards him, he fell. Two ambulance men ran out with a stretcher. Paul was seized roughly by a fireman and ordered back.

As he was pushed unceremoniously out of the circle of rescuers, he caught a glimpse of a woman remonstrating with the fire chief. Undeterred, she ran towards the ambulance just as it was moving off.

Tony Blair woke slowly, painfully. Someone seemed to be sitting on his leg. He tried to move it and winced in agony.

'You all right, mate?' asked a voice from a million miles away.

'What happened?' said Blair.

'You flaked out when you hit the deck,' Mason said. He grinned. 'But you've only broken a leg. You'll live.'

'And you?'

'A few bruises,' Mason said. 'Pete's bust his nose, but it suits him.'

'And what about the Old Lady?' Blair asked sleepily.

'Feeling a bit sorry for herself,' Mason said. 'But I reckon if we can scratch a few quid together, we can get her back on her feet sometime.'

'I thought she'd given up the ghost,' Blair said.

Mason laughed. 'Not yet, mate. She's a right old buccaneer, that one.'

Blair smiled back. Slowly he began to focus his eyes on the ceiling. It looked vaguely familiar. That big spreading patch of yellow where the cistern had burst one year and he had never got round to having it repapered. It always reminded him of the map of Africa.

'Where am I?' he asked.

'You're home,' Janet said, and took his hand.